Convictions

bitlit

A **free** eBook edition is available
with the purchase of this print book.

Convictions

JUDITH SILVERTHORNE

COTEAU BOOKS

Edited by Kathryn Cole
Book designed by Tania Craan
Typeset by Susan Buck
Printed and bound in Canada

Library and Archives Canada Cataloguing in Publication

Silverthorne, Judith, author
          Convictions / Judith Silverthorne.

Issued in print and electronic formats.
ISBN 978-1-55050-652-5 (paperback).--ISBN 978-1-55050-653-2 (pdf).--
ISBN 978-1-55050-889-5 (html).--ISBN 978-1-55050-890-1 (html)

          I. Title.

PS8587.I2763C65 2016   jC813'.54   C2015-908760-0
                                                 C2015-908761-9

Library of Congress Control Number: 2015954154

2517 Victoria Avenue
Regina, Saskatchewan
Canada S4P 0T2
www.coteaubooks.com

Available in Canada from:
Publishers Group Canada
2440 Viking Way
Richmond, British Columbia
Canada V6V 1N2

10 9 8 7 6 5 4 3 2 1

Coteau Books gratefully acknowledges the financial support of its publishing program by: the Saskatchewan Arts Board, The Canada Council for the Arts, the Government of Saskatchewan through Creative Saskatchewan, the City of Regina. We further acknowledge the [financial] support of the Government of Canada. Nous reconnaissons l'appui [financier] du gouvernement du Canada.

To all the truly wonderful women in my life,

who stand strong in their convictions.

AUTHOR'S NOTE

Ships carrying convicts destined for North America ceased in 1776 when the War of Independence broke out in the United States. However, the practice of transporting felons continued to the penal colonies in Australia and New Zealand for about another ninety years, the numbers totaling 162,000 men and women. Exclusively female convict ships were infrequent – 129 out of a total of 806 – but they did sail, especially after facts emerged about the particularly harsh and sordid conditions women suffered on co-gendered transport ships.

One such exclusively female convict ship called the *Mary Anne* sailed in 1840, another called the *Emily* a couple of years later. The fictitious name of the ship in this story, the *Emily Anne*, is a combination of the two, sailing in 1842 for Van Diemen's Land (Tasmania), Australia. Real facts, the strife of real people, and the conditions of actual convict ships form the foundation for this story.

CONVICTION

1350–1400; (v.) Middle English convicten
1400–50; late Middle English < Late Latin conviction-
(stem of convicti) proof (of guilt).

DEFINITION:

- *a fixed or firm belief*

- *an unshakable belief in something without need for proof or evidence*

- *acknowledgement; strong persuasion or belief; condemnation*

- *the act of convincing of error, or of compelling the admission of a truth; confutation.*

- *the state of being convinced or convicted; strong persuasion or belief; especially, the state of being convicted of sin, or by one's conscience.*

- *a judgment of condemnation entered by a court having jurisdiction; the act or process of finding guilty, or the state of being found guilty of any crime by a legal tribunal.*

- *the act of proving, finding, or adjudging, guilty of an offense.*

- *(criminal law) a final judgment of guilty in a criminal case and the punishment that is imposed*

- *to prove or declare guilty of an offense, especially after a legal trial: to convict a prisoner of a felony.*

- *to impress with a sense of guilt*

CHAPTER ONE

JUNE 29, 1842

JENNIE'S BARE FEET burned as she stepped down onto the sun-baked cobblestones from the crammed prison wagon, one of many lined three deep next to the Liverpool quay. She swallowed hard at the sudden cloying stench of dead fish, rotting wood and slime. Sweat beaded on her forehead in the glaring noonday sun. She brushed fingers across her face and wiped them on the tattered dress that clung to her thin body.

A guard yanked her by the shoulders. She winced as he cuffed her wrists behind her back. A second guard snapped shackles on her ankles and then thrust her behind ten year old Alice. The girl huddled against Jennie until a third guard chained them to an already-formed line. In silence, they waited for the rest of the female convicts to join the fettered queue. Quaking inside, Jennie ran her dry tongue over parched lips.

Whips crackled overhead, and at last the line of emaciated women lurched forward along the crowded wharf. With slow, uneven steps, Jennie trekked with the other prisoners. Many kept their heads down as they edged past the throng of onlookers waiting with friends and family to board their respective passenger ships. With each hobbled step toward the ship bound for Van Diemen, the heavy manacles bit into Jennie's ankles.

"Be gone with you, ya thieving women," someone hollered.

"Yeah, good riddance!" yelled a tall man whose head stuck above the crowd.

Jennie tensed as he pushed his way toward them.

"You're good for nothing rubbish, and we're best rid of your kind," he snarled. "If anyone disagrees, they belong on the convict ship with you." His spittle landed near Jennie's bare feet.

"Shut your yap!" someone else bellowed.

"Make me," the tall heckler roared and turned toward the voice.

"It'll give me pleasure!" A young punter pushed his way through the horde.

The tall man lunged, but someone tripped him. Jennie cringed as he caught himself before falling into her. He flailed his fists at those in his vicinity. The crowd cut him a wide berth.

"Leave 'em alone. They're paying for their crimes," a squat man in a top hat harrumphed.

Dissenting shouts rose. A scuffle broke out in the middle of the mass.

"Some of them are only children," a woman near Jennie said in surprise.

"They'll grow up without their families," said another.

The horror of her destiny closed in on Jennie. She stumbled, and the ankle chains bit harder into her skin.

The group of hecklers swarmed closer, crushing past bystanders waving good-bye to loved ones who were boarding a nearby ship. The wooden wharf creaked under the added weight. Amid the shoving and cursing, a well-dressed lady screamed when she was shoved to the ground. As her husband picked her up, their child started crying.

Jennie twisted to see.

"Keep back," yelled a wharf policeman, charging toward the crowd.

"They'll push us off," wailed an older convict farther down the line.

"Are we going to die?" Alice whimpered in front of Jennie.

"Sh. We'll be all right," Jennie said. "I have an eye out for you."

The shouting grew louder as more people joined the fray. Overhead, screaming seagulls wheeled against the cloudless sky, plunging for scraps from a row of waterside fish stalls. Police whistles shrieked.

A sudden volley of gunshots exploded over the heads of the crowd. Everything stopped at once.

Then, as if in slow motion, people righted themselves. Officers pushed through the crowd looking for troublemakers and the injured.

The guards flicked their whips overhead to get the line moving again. The heavy manacles bit deeper into Jennie's wrists and ankles as they approached their vessel moored farther down the wharf.

Jennie watched as the line of women bobbed along the quay like a string of fishing boats nodding in the wind. Young and old, fit and maimed, some pregnant and some children as young as seven were bound together. Many youngsters and babes in arms were with their condemned mothers, Jennie knew, only because there was no one left to care for them at home. She had spent time in prison with some of them over the past four months. Many more Jennie did not know, as they had been transported from across the whole of Great Britain, some even from Ireland.

The leaden chains and the unseasonably warm weather were almost more than Jennie could bear. The brisk wind mingling with the briny tang of salt water did little to ease her distress. Jennie had no idea which of the three-masted vessels

3

along the quay would carry her so far from home.

She searched desperately through the throng for her mother. Had she not found a way to come? Didn't she know this was probably the last time Jennie could ever hope to see her?

"Move on!" A burly guard with a bushy red moustache and beard shoved someone a few feet ahead of her, setting off a chain reaction of falling women.

Jennie lurched forward, smashing headlong into Alice. Pain seared her wrists, as other women fell against her. A chin dug into her back, and with her face planted between Alice's narrow shoulders, Jennie couldn't breathe.

"Sorry, dearie," said the matronly woman behind her.

Managing to stand upright once more, Jennie felt nauseated as she gasped and smelled the stench of dead fish and decaying seaweed. She swallowed hard.

"Can you manage?" the stout woman from behind asked.

Jennie nodded, though she felt weaker than she had ever been on her hungriest days. Taking shallow breaths through her mouth, she managed to hold back the nausea.

"We'll soon be out of this heat," the woman added.

Jennie glanced back and murmured, "Thank you."

"Sarah Givens. From London. Chimney sweep's wife. Seven children, youngest nine," she puffed. Wisps of brown frizzy hair clung to her plump face.

Jennie spoke over her shoulder. "I'm Jennie – uh – Mary Jane Lawrence. My family calls me Jennie. I'm most recent from Manchester, before that Warrington."

"You're young."

"Fourteen, last month," Jennie said. She pushed back her shoulders.

"Same age as my Susan."

Through further snippets of whispering, Jennie learned that Sarah Given's sentence stemmed from a false accusation of stealing a handkerchief. She had been returning it to the owner, who had dropped it as she alighted from a carriage.

"You can be sure I won't be so obliging next time," said Sarah.

The red-bearded guard stormed toward them.

"No talkin', you. Eyes straight ahead!"

He prodded Jennie in the chest with a stick. She clamped her mouth shut, her face burned with shame.

Jennie moved along, staring straight ahead for several moments before peeking upwards. Hundreds of masts and spars prodded the sky. She would soon be on one of the tall vessels. This really was the end of the only life she knew. What would happen to her when they landed in Van Diemen's Land some four or five months from now? A jolt of terror shot through her.

If only her family hadn't been hungry. If only she had not been so desperate to find something for them to eat, she would never have taken the sack of oats – a discarded mouldy sack at that.

Passengers, sailors, merchants and dockworkers hustled along the pier, dodging Jennie and the long string of women, passing goods over their heads when they couldn't go around. As the women threaded their way around stacked crates and bales of tobacco and silk, Jennie caught the welcome scent of tea and spices.

Farther along, cows, goats, sheep and horses were prodded from holding pens. Jennie watched dockworkers secure the livestock one at a time into a four-bellyband harness. With a boom that swung from the quay, they hoisted the livestock up and over, then lowered the bellowing beasts through a top cargo hatch into the hold. Jennie knew how the animals felt.

Behind her, the red-bearded guard laughed. "Mates, look at this fat 'un. Can't even stand up proper."

Jennie glanced back in disgust as he shoved his stick into the chains between Sarah Givens' feet and twisted.

Sarah almost pulled others down with her, but Jennie and

the woman behind Sarah wedged themselves to hold her upright. Little Alice clutched at Jennie.

Still chuckling, the guard continued up the line. Jennie glanced over her shoulder, but another guard was coming up behind them.

"I'm all right," the stout woman assured Jennie in a loud whisper. Under her breath Jennie was sure she heard Sarah mutter, "Bloody Cockney bastard."

A whip cracked near Jennie. She recoiled. The line lurched when the guard struck someone with a club. Alice cried out as the guards continued poking and prodding the women.

Suddenly, the progression stopped.

Sarah said, "This is it then."

Jennie craned her neck to see ahead. Others did the same, whispering.

"Silence!" yelled a scar-faced guard standing near the ramp to the ship. "Your turn to board will come soon enough!"

Beside them, a dark hulk was moored parallel to the wharf. Jennie shuddered. The *Emily Anne* would be her prison for the duration of the sea voyage.

As those at the front of the line began their ascent, the flimsy wooden gangplank rocked. The women shuffled forward a little, then stopped again. Moved. Stopped. The sporadic progress seemed to go on forever under the baking sun. One by one, the guards directed the women onto the swaying gangway. Jennie's fear increased with each step.

Around her, ankle shackles and chains clanked. Tackles and pulleys screeched as shouting dockworkers loaded the last crates and barrels of provisions onto the vessels. Heartfelt shouts of good-bye from family members all along the wharf merged with officers' sharp commands to sailors. Warders hollered directions to the convicts. Every sound clanged in Jennie's head, until she thought she'd explode.

She scanned the crowd again. Had her mother really not come? Jennie's steps faltered. The gangway wobbled as she stepped onto it and pitched against the rope railing.

"Steady," Sarah whispered.

Jennie's legs stiffened with each step up the ramp. She pushed away the tales that had been whispered in prison. Those about harsh discipline and deadly sickness of convicts transported to the colonies. When she spotted the soldiers with guns leaning over the poop deck railing above them, she shivered. She forced images of home to crowd out the horrors she imagined.

She thought of her mother's kind face and the laughter they shared with her two sisters in the tiny room above a milliner's shop. It was not much more than a storeroom that her mother had found after her father's death, but at least they had been warm and dry. The small fireplace offered a place to cook their meagre meals and gave them some warmth from the scavenged coal they burned in the winter months. The family had been safe and together, unlike many others who had lost the main wage earner in the household.

If she hadn't stolen from the rubbish bin, they would all be safe at home now – her mother, her eleven-year-old sister, Beth, and herself – hand-sewing throughout the day with eight-year-old Ann helping as best she could. They would continue long into the night, long after Ann fell sound asleep on the straw pallet she shared with their mother. Jennie would miss cuddling next to Beth for warmth at night. If only they had been able to find another outlet to sell their finely stitched gloves and handkerchiefs – some outlet where the seller would not cheat them out of their pay.

Jennie's footsteps dragged behind Alice's trembling body as she neared the top of the long, narrow ramp. One more step and she'd be severed from her family, perhaps forever. Even if her sentence was only for seven years, how would she be able to return? What would become of her family while she was gone? Her stomach reeled and her knees almost gave way. What would become of *her?*

She had to see her mother one last time. Jennie pulled up short, causing another chain reaction and groans of dismay. The gangplank rocked.

"Get on with ya!" ordered a thin warder with a face like a wizened apple.

Jennie clamped her toes onto the bare wood, straining to scan the crowded quay. Was her mother there?

Whack!

Jennie's shoulder flared with pain. The red-bearded guard raised his wooden club to strike again. The wizened-faced warder grinned.

Alice whimpered and crouched down. Sarah stood in shock.

"Move!" the bull-like guard roared, his red beard bristling. He shoved Jennie toward the deck. She stumbled but clung to the rope. She couldn't go without seeing her mother. Jennie leaned hard into the rope, shaking.

The "Red Bull" pushed her again.

"Wait!" she shouted.

Startled, the guard paused.

In that instant, Jennie glimpsed the distraught figure of her mother, moving a little apart from the others. Her tiny frame seemed shrunken. She clutched Jennie's dark-haired sisters to her as if they were the only things keeping her upright.

Jennie held her head high and looked into her mother's eyes. Ada Lawrence spoke to her younger daughters and they immediately stood tall, though tears streaked down their faces. Jennie nodded. Her mother, holding a white handkerchief, reached out her hand in a futile gesture. That was the last Jennie saw of her family before Red Bull shoved her again, and she plunged face down onto the deck.

CHAPTER TWO

JENNIE'S KNEES SMARTED as she fell. Her face scraped along the rough wooden deck. Behind her, Sarah and the other linked convicts tumbled along the pitching gangplank. The women grumbled and swore as they clung to the swaying ropes.

Red Bull snatched Jennie up and smacked her across the face.

"Try sommat like that again, and ye'll regret it," he snarled. He yanked the women behind her to their feet.

Jennie's mouth quivered. She ran her tongue over her lips and tasted blood.

The wizened-faced guard wrenched off Jennie's two sets of shackles. "Git over there." He indicated the spot beside Alice.

The young girl stood uncertainly next to the mainmast near the captain's cabin, her face awash with shock. Jennie strained to keep back tears as she shuffled unsteadily through the tangle of ropes. With a shaky hand, she wiped her mouth.

The guard moved on to Sarah. He unfettered her and shoved her beside Jennie. Sarah clucked quietly. Without a word, she used the hem of her dress to wipe the blood off Jennie's split lip.

One by one, the restraints came off each prisoner. As they appeared on board the women lined up again, next to Alice, Jennie and Sarah. Jennie massaged her bruised wrists, avoiding the worst chafed spots. Her ankles hurt too, but her mouth throbbed the most.

In a stupor, she stared across the harbour, watching fishing boats bobbing their way down the River Mersey toward Liverpool Bay and thence into the Irish Sea. After that it was the vast nothingness of the Atlantic Ocean and a life Jennie couldn't begin to fathom.

A swarthy warder with a scar across the left side of his face strode up to Jennie, his fetid breath hot on her face. He pawed at her dress and down her front with beefy fingers, muttering about searching for knives, matches or any other dangerous instrument she might have.

Jennie froze. She knew she had to submit or endure being struck again. But she couldn't stop the wave of panic that pressed against her chest.

"Can never be too careful with the likes of you," the guard leered. When his pudgy hands squeezed her bottom, his eyes lit with the pleasure of humiliating her.

She forced herself to stand as still as stone. To keep her revulsion at bay, her mind struggled through memories of her family – anything to block out the horrible assault on her body from this scar-faced man. But the panic rose from her stomach, almost making her choke, when he squeezed her breasts. A terrified, mewling sound escaped from her throat.

She jerked her head and caught sight of a young guard standing near the hatchway. His face reddened and his brown eyes filled with an expression she couldn't name – anger, pity, disgust.

Scarface leered again as he clutched Jennie's bottom one last time. Then he motioned her farther along the deck to where an older thin man with a shock of grey hair and spectacles sat at a small wooden table.

"Inspection. Give him your name, and be quick." The scar-faced guard pushed Jennie forward, then reached for Sarah.

Legs like wood, Jennie shuffled to stand in front of the seated man. Her throat tightened so much she could barely mumble her name.

"Another Mary! You must be the twentieth one so far. Don't know how you'll keep yourselves straight!" The older man peered at his sheet and made a tick.

"I'm Mary Jane, called Jennie at home," she said, but he ignored her response.

"Do a full turn." He twirled his index finger in a quick circle without looking up.

Jennie rotated with halting steps until she faced him again. He hardly glanced at her, not even noticing her split lip and scraped face. He pointed her toward the opening into the black depths of the ship.

Jennie willed herself forward, but her feet wouldn't move. Her mind went blank.

"You agen," a voice growled close to her ear.

She felt a sharp prod in her back. Glancing quickly over her shoulder, she saw Red Bull with a smirk on his face.

"Keep this up an' it will be a restricted cell with plenty of beatings for ya."

Then a gentle, but firm hand touched her arm.

"Come, luv. We must be strong." Sarah led her forward. "We'll see this through together."

The kind words shook Jennie out of her paralysis. She moved toward the dark hatch. Already she could feel the stifling heat rising. With one last deep breath of salty sea air, Jennie sank into the belly of the ship. Halfway down, one foot slipped and she scraped her already painful ankle against the edge of a wooden rung. The added injury brought her to full attention. She'd never felt so miserable. Tears prickled at her eyelids.

At first, after the bright sunlight outside, Jennie couldn't see much of anything in the steerage hold. Around her, she could hear the sounds of moving bodies, rustling clothes and shuffling feet. And she was sure she heard the scrabbling of rats. The rough talk of the guards and orders for the crew coming from the dark void added to her bewilderment.

Although several candlelit lanterns hung along the centre passageway, very little light managed to press through the few grimy portholes. And those were barred like the windows of a prison. The constant rocking of the boat kept Jennie off balance. Voices around her cried out in alarm and uncertainty as she and her companions stumbled along in the gloom.

Guards stationed at intervals along the passageway prodded them with muskets, as the women lurched against one another. Someone pushed Alice sideways, crushing her into two sinewy women. Jennie pulled her free. Alice clung to Jennie's arm, as Sarah drew them both toward her.

"Order!" yelled a formidable voice above the din.

All attention focused on the dark, commanding form of a uniformed officer, who hung partway down the ladder.

When all became quiet, he shouted, "I am Lieutenant Yates, second in command. I speak on behalf of Captain Furlee, master of this vessel. He will tolerate no disorder on board. Now give heed. We intend to arrive with all two hundred and thirty-five of you. Your condition at that time depends entirely on how you behave."

He pointed to another officer farther down the rungs. "Second Mate Meadows is in charge to see that you do. He will give further orders." Yates disappeared up the narrow ladder as swiftly as he'd come.

Meadows climbed up a few steps, his tall muscular body filling the space where the Lieutenant had been. He bellowed, "Reverend Ernest Brantford is here for your spiritual redemption."

Jennie pressed through the crowd of women until she could glimpse the stick-like man with bony hands and long narrow skull Meadows indicated, standing at the bottom of the ladder to the right. The tight, white collar around the reverend's neck prevented him from giving more than a slight nod in their direction. Jennie shivered. He resembled a skeleton that she'd seen once in the back of an apothecary shop.

"The surgery," Meadows said, signalling two warders to hold lanterns inside a small ten-by-twelve-foot space near the hatchway.

Jennie craned to see inside. Equipped with six bed planks and a cradle, there was also a table, a chair, and a narrow shelf against the far wall which held quart bottles containing powders of some sort.

A man stepped forward as Meadows bellowed an introduction. "Once we set sail Surgeon Superintendent Dr. Weymss will choose three of you as his attendants. You will do his bidding." The surgeon was the man who had taken their names above deck. He was shorter than Jennie had thought, now that he was standing.

"Over there are the privies." Meadows indicated four wooden buckets, two on each side of a plank. "You will see to their emptying."

Around her, the women gasped. Jennie shuddered – there weren't nearly enough to serve all of them!

All became silent when Meadows bellowed again to get their attention.

"Take note of the brig at the far end." He pointed his sword over their heads toward jail cells. "You will join your unruly companions there, should you become disobedient. So be fairly warned."

Someone whispered behind Jennie. "Behind them's where the second-rate officers that looks after the ship stays."

"The gun room is back there too," rasped someone else. "And where the guards have their berths."

"Aye, and look. The dividing wall has holes for the guards to fire on us if we get rowdy," said the first woman.

"Too close for my comfort," said the other.

A rustle of muttering swept through the hold, but ceased when Meadows commanded, "Hold your noise!"

He further focused their attention with his cutting words. "You'll remain chained below deck until we've set sail and reached open water. You'll receive further orders then."

Meadows signalled again to the warders. "Nate and Walt, take the lanterns and call the others to get these women in their berths forthwith."

So the young warder's name is Nate, Jennie noted. And right behind him, walking with a slight limp, was Walt, the man with the wizened face. Jennie kept her head slightly bowed as Nate, ramrod straight, headed her way. His expression was hard to read, obscured as it was by the glare of the lamp he held at arm's length.

Before her in the shadowy light, Jennie could just make out a row of berths divided into wards, running the length of four or five portholes on each side of the ship. Iron bars divided the wards into square sections with two tiers of bunks in each. The bunks didn't look much wider than Jennie with both her arms stretched out at her sides.

"Four of you in each," snarled Scarface. He steered a group of women into the nearest lower berth and handcuffed them to the vertical metal bars. "The last of you will take the hammocks," he shouted over his shoulder.

The women crowded forward, scrambling to make sure they found a berth space. The hammocks were gnarled and frayed and had no mattresses. Each was meant for at least two, and no one wanted to share and be rolled into the middle together when it sagged.

Sarah tottered ahead of Jennie and Alice. She grasped at the first open bunk she came to with space for all of them, but it was on the second level several feet off the ground. Alice scampered up, but the middle-aged woman looked down at her bulk.

"I'll never get up there," she wheezed.

Jennie helped her companion into the next bottom bunk that already held three other women in a space barely meant for two. As Sarah wedged herself onto the plank berth, the others grumbled about her girth.

"You can surely move in tighter," Sarah gasped. She clung to the edge of the bunk, her body threatening to roll off.

"Wish we could get you in here too, Jennie," she grunted, her face flushed.

"That's fine, I'll go up with Alice." But by that time, Alice was squashed against the far wall of her berth by three others who had joined her.

Jennie tried to enter the lower one next to Sarah, but a stout grey-haired woman dug her fingers into Jennie's arm.

"You're young. Go to the top," she ordered, before ducking back into the bottom compartment where there was still some space.

Jennie gave her a look of surprise, and began to climb. A pockmarked, gangly woman in her mid-twenties thrust her foot out from above.

"There's no room," she growled, though there was only one other youngish woman with her.

Jennie recognized them both as the ones Alice had been crushed into earlier.

"Yes, there is," she said, climbing upward again.

"Not for the prissy likes of you!"

Jennie slid back down. With the throng of woman surrounding her, there seemed nowhere else for her to go and still be near Sarah and Alice.

A fight erupted between the women farther along the passageway.

"Only the elderly and mothers with babies and children are allowed the bottom bunks," bellowed Walt, separating the tangle of women. He shoved them in opposite directions. "Make room."

Jennie attempted to climb up again, but the other tough woman – a scraggly blonde – joined the pockmarked one in blocking her ascent.

"We'll have none of that, lest you want a flogging." Scarface approached from the other direction with a snarl, smacking his billy club at the obstinate women. He grabbed Jennie and lifted her up by the waist, thrusting her into the adjoining upper bunk amidst three sweaty bodies. The three others complained loudly, as they disentangled arms and legs. Jabbing Jennie, they pushed her to the back. She moaned, feeling every injury anew. The guard stepped on the edge of the bottom bunk and stretched over to snap handcuffs on their wrists, securing them to the metal bars at their heads.

Jennie squirmed to get comfortable on her side, though she was squished tight against the wall. She took several anxious breaths. The constant swaying of the ship lapping at its moorings helped calm her, as did concentrating on listening to the rest of the women find berths along the full length of the ward section. Finally, everyone seemed to have eked out a space, the last claiming the tatty hammocks. The guards finished handcuffing them in place and secured the threadbare lee cloths meant to keep them from rolling out of their bunks.

With the dousing of the lanterns, the sounds in their quarters dulled to murmurs, broken only by the occasional baby's cry or whimper from a child and several hoarsely whispered prayers. From the jail-cell end came the sobbing of a woman who seemed unable to stop.

Jennie lay rammed into the narrow berth with her bedmates. The thin straw pallet did little to cushion her injured body. Her shoulders and back were in pain from the clubbing, and her ankles and wrists throbbed. Every muscle in her body ached. There was no pillow, only a threadbare blanket, which she pulled up to her chin, careful not to touch her swollen jaw.

A bony elbow dug into her ribs, and the smell of unwashed bodies was overwhelming. Jennie cowered away from the other women, pressing tightly against the hull of the ship. She squirmed suddenly when she felt something nibbling at her legs. She couldn't reach to scratch with her hands. She brushed her legs against one another in small movements, praying she'd be able to knock off the bedbugs or spiders or whatever crawled on her.

"Quit fidgeting!" The woman beside Jennie poked her.

Weak and queasy, Jennie closed her eyes, trying to ignore the crawling bugs. She listened to the crews hollering orders as they prepared the ship for sailing. At the other end of steerage, a deck below them, the livestock bellowed and bleated. Men cursed as they lashed the last of the cargo into place.

A cannon shot thundered from somewhere overhead. Shortly afterwards, Jennie heard shouted orders to hoist the sails. Moments later, the ship trembled into life.

Jennie's eyes sprang open as the ship tilted and then swayed back again. She lay paralyzed, staring wide-eyed into the dark void, listening to the groaning of the ship. Then a bell clanged, sounding like a death knell.

June 29, 1842 was a date she would never forget.

CHAPTER THREE

Darkness engulfed her.

Moaning softly, Jennie pressed harder against the rough hull, away from the women sharing her berth. Although she was surrounded by women, they were strangers and she'd never felt so alone. The dank, cramped bowels of the ship closed in on her. This was worse than anything she had imagined.

The ship's creaking, the bumping and bawling of the cattle below and peculiar banging noises mingled with shouts of the sailors above board horrified her. Even more, the terrified whispers of her companions, the furtive scratching of rodents and the rocking of the ship created an overwhelming sense of danger.

Everything seemed to be closing in on her. The berth was like a shared coffin. The sweaty bodies in her berth smacked against each other with a scant eighteen inches to call their own. Even if Jennie could turn on her other side, the space was too shallow; the ceiling only few inches from her face. Desperation crept through her as she thought about the horror of spending the next four or five months in these confined, coal-black depths.

Her breathing came in short, quick bursts. In a panic, Jennie jerked upwards on one elbow. She whacked her forehead on the top beam. The short wrist fetter yanked her down again, and she cracked the back of her head against an iron bar. She yelped and gulped back sobs.

"Hush her up, Hildy," said the woman lying two positions over.

"Stuff it, Flo. Why should it be me?" Hildy griped.

"You're closest."

Jennie whimpered again.

"Give 'er a slap," said the youngest woman on the outside of the berth. "That'll stop the bleedin' 'ysterics!"

"Give her one yourself, Gladys," Hildy snapped, as she butted her bony shoulder against Jennie. "Stop the whining or you'll have the billy clubs down on us."

"Shh. Don't distress yourself, dearie," Sarah comforted from a berth below. "It's of no use."

"I'm scared too." Alice's trembling voice reached Jennie's ears.

Jennie felt ashamed of herself. Alice had to be even more terrified than she was. She took in a long quavering breath to steady herself.

"Don't mind me, Alice. I'm better now." Jennie tried to reassure the youngster, though her heart pounded hard against her chest.

"We'll get through this together," Sarah promised, as Alice choked back a sob. "Don't fret now, Alice. I'm close by."

Jennie added hollowly, "We'll come out right."

"Hmmph," grunted Hildy.

"Shows how little she knows," muttered Flo.

"All we have now is our prayers," said someone with the high-pitched voice directly below Jennie.

"Is that you, Iris? Fat lot of good prayers 'ave done," Gladys scoffed. "Look where they've brought us!"

"Prayers work. You must believe," Iris said, her voice rising indignantly.

"Imagine where we'd be if the prayers *didn't* work," Flo scoffed.

"We'd be swinging from the three-legged mare," barked an elderly voice.

"Cheerful ruddy thought that, Dottie!" said Hildy with a sniff.

"At least we can be thankful that's not our fate," said Sarah.

"It'd be better than living in this stinking hole," volleyed back one of the tough young women from the bunk next to Jennie's head.

"Come now, Lizzie, we must have *Christian fortitude!*" Iris's voice rose an octave.

"If the bloody Lord *is* around, why doesn't he save us from this cruelty?" Gladys demanded.

The bickering continued between those who felt their religion had failed them and those who clung to a stalwart belief in a merciful God. Jennie listened and her stomach clenched. How could people talk like this? This was heresy. She could hear her mother's voice: "Don't ever take the Lord's name in vain." The Lord's Prayer flitted through her mind. Silently she began praying.

"Stop your waggin' tongues," a warder sounding like Scarface shouted close by.

A weak glow of light wavered by Jennie's berth.

Bang!

Gladys yelped.

"Keep your body parts out of the aisle," Scarface warned. He continued in the direction of the surgery, banging his club against the berths as he passed.

Voices quieted, but the ship's sounds magnified from different corners in the dark. Jennie quaked with fear. Not only had she entered a terrifying unknown, but she had never questioned her faith before.

Now she began to wonder about the events of her life. She'd

prayed for food, and when she'd found the sack of musty oats in the rubbish bin, she thought it was the answer to that prayer. Would the forgiving God she'd trusted all her life let her and her family suffer and almost starve to death? Was this terrible punishment a retribution or a test of her faith? The more she thought about it, the more agitated she became.

The warder passed again, heading back toward the gun-room, still banging his club. Laughter erupted from inside the room at the end of the passage as he opened the door. He closed it again, but not before Jennie heard the shuffling of cards and the clanking of coins on a table and the unmistakable voice of Red Bull, saying, "Oi'll raise you three shillings." Jennie felt her skin crawl.

"Already gambling, and we haven't even made it out of the harbour," scoffed Hildy.

"You're just jealous, Hildy, wishing you were playing," snickered someone from below.

"Shut your yap, Mary," said Hildy.

"Who are you telling to shut up?" said a new voice.

"I didn't mean you, Mary *Cavanaugh*," said Hildy.

"What about me, then? You referring to me?" someone else asked.

"I don't know your voice. Who are you, then?" asked Hildy.

"Mary. Mary *Pilling*."

"No, I meant you Mary, whatever your last name is below me," Hildy said in exasperation.

The woman responded, "I'm Mary Roberts if you must know, and I don't take kindly to you telling me to shut up, either."

"Nor do I," said another voice. "Mary Breck here."

Several more up and down the passageway shouted "Mary" along with their last names.

"How many bloomin' Marys are on this tub?" asked Gladys.

"Too many!" Hildy muttered under her breath so that only

Jennie could hear.

Jennie drew in a breath. "I'm a Mary too," she said in a low voice.

"Blimey! All you Marys better sort *yourselfs* out." Hildy ended in a shout. "You'll drive us barmy keeping you straight."

"I go by Jennie."

"I'm a Molly," said someone from the far end.

More began reeling off their nicknames – "Meg, May, Millie –"

"Enough already!" said Hildy. "We can't even see you to put faces to!"

"Well, at least we know if we call for Mary, someone will answer," Gladys chortled.

"Fine lot of good that'll do," Hildy grunted.

Abruptly the gunroom door banged open against the wall and a guard bellowed, "That's enough out of all of you, Marys or no!"

Scarface was silhouetted in the doorway. He whacked his stick against the nearest bunk. "A body can't get any rest with you lot. Now shut your yaps, or it will be beatings for yous next." From behind him came shouts of agreement and the clink of tin cups on tables. He slammed the door shut again, and the air snapped with sudden silence.

Hildy ventured a whisper. "Guess we did get a little loud, if they heard us over their gamblin' and rum drinkin'."

"That why you're here again, Hildy? Gambling?" Gladys asked in a low, husky voice.

"Mebbe," murmured Hildy.

"Helped yerself too liberally to the winnings, maybe?" offered Gladys in a snide undertone.

"Give off airing me filthy knickers, or I'll give over how you pull fast ones on nobs at the theatres," Hildy hissed.

"You're just jealous of my expert sleight of hand," cackled Gladys softly.

"You're no better than Lizzie at *shopping*," Fanny cracked, her voice rising above a whisper.

"Shh," someone scolded.

Gladys whispered loud enough so those in their bunk could hear. "Maybe, but at least I didn't get made for trouncing a copper, like Lizzie did."

"Why are you bringing me into this?" growled Lizzie from the next bunk. "Besides, he deserved it, didn't he then. He wanted the stuff for hisself."

"Must have been worth a lot, then, if you risked this fate," Hildy said.

"Would have been, had I managed to keep it," Lizzie grumbled. "How about you? Was the risk worth this again?"

"Not in coins, but I *will* get to see my Dickie again," said Hildy smugly. "There was no way he was ever coming back home. He got done for eighteen years."

Jennie listened, surprised at Hildy's explanation for committing a crime in order to be reunited with her husband. An unexpected emptiness clutched at Jennie's stomach as she wondered how her family was managing without her. One less mouth to feed to be sure, but also one less pair of hands to bear the work and figure out how best to make ends meet. She hoped her mum and sisters wouldn't have to go to the dreaded workhouse.

"What about you then, Flo?" asked Gladys.

"I *borrowed* a horse," Flo answered. "But I returned it," she insisted, "only the owners didn't quite see it that way." She sighed. "Fanny, you must have a right good story to tell us. I haven't seen you done up for a long while."

"Stole a wallet from a *gentleman*." Fanny guffawed. Several laughed.

Jennie recognized the voice of the pockmarked woman, who lay in the berth next to her head beside Lizzie – the other mean woman who wouldn't let her into the berth. All of the women speaking seemed to know each other in some way; together in jail at one time or another, she figured.

"The toff chirped. Though 'e was wadded up and could 'ave spared it," Fanny added.

Lizzie chided, "You're such a doxy, Fanny!"

Jennie blushed at the crude word. She'd overheard her mother refer to the women walking under the street lamps late at night as doxies, but she had never met one before. Nor did she know what they did.

Suddenly, Fanny kicked the bars at Jennie's head. "And how's about your crime, Miss Prim?"

Jennie didn't want to tell anyone why she was on the ship. Fanny kicked harder.

"Please stop," said Jennie. She tried to stall. "We'll get a beating."

Bang! Fanny slammed her foot near Jennie's head again. "Then speak up!"

"Oats," Jennie whispered, hoping, because they were all in the dark, no one would know who spoke. She was so humiliated by what she'd done. She wasn't like all the others, not really. She was a good girl.

"Louder!"

"I stole a sack of oats the milliner's wife threw away." Jennie spoke louder and finished in a rush, not wanting the guards to hear Fanny's commotion and hoping the questions would end. She also didn't want to recall the terrible ordeal.

"Aren't you're a brave one then, stealing out of a dustbin," Fanny said sarcastically.

Jennie felt the heat rush into her face.

"There's no call to be offensive, Fanny," Iris said. "We're decent folk, unlike you."

"Decent folk?" Fanny scoffed. "Where do you think you *are*,

Iris? On a voyage for an exotic holiday with toffs? Stealing sugar for your dying dad's tea is still theft!"

From beside Fanny, Lizzie said, "Yeah, you're here with us, ain't ya? Call us doxies or whatever names you like. But you're no better than us. None of you."

Jennie sucked in her breath as the words sank in. Surely stealing a sack of discarded oats couldn't make her as bad as... as a *doxy*. Neither could she be lumped in with the "real" criminals, could she? But no one looking at them now would know the difference. That was what being on this ship meant. She was branded a criminal for life. Shame engulfed her.

Iris's high voice crackled out of the void. "We're all equal in the eyes of the Lord."

"You got that right, at least," said Fanny. "And you'll all be doing the same thing as us when we reach Van Diemen's Land."

Gladys groaned. "Ooh, don't say that."

"There's not much other choice, I hear tell," said Flo quietly.

"That'll even us up all the more," chuckled Lizzie.

Jennie froze. What were they talking about? Her mother had never told her why she disapproved of doxies, but it didn't sound pleasant.

As the whispering subsided, Jennie pressed against the hull and tried to sleep. But the conversations kept running through her head.

What *was* she going to have to do? Whatever that was, she knew it couldn't be good.

CHAPTER FOUR

THE SOUND OF RETCHING interrupted Jennie's fretful sleep. She turned her head away from the acrid smell.

"Gladys, are you all right?" Hildy's elbow dug into Jennie as she pushed up to see their bunkmate on the outside edge.

Gladys moaned.

"Guards!" Hildy called. She rattled her manacles up and down the iron bar. "Someone's ailing."

"I don't feel well either," moaned Flo.

"Nor me," screeched Iris.

"Help! Guard!" Hildy yelled, before she too heaved.

Jennie recoiled, as Hildy's mess splattered on her.

"Bloody hell, the seasickness has started already," yelled Red Bull, bursting out of the guard room. "We need lanterns."

Scarface, Nate and Walt scurried to unfasten the lee cloths and unlock the handcuffs from those who were heaving nearby.

Jennie closed her eyes and tried not to breathe. Cries for immediate attention rose up and down the passageway amid the sounds of others spewing. The sour biting odour made Jennie think of her grandmother, who'd died of cholera less than a year before. Jennie was the one to find her, lying ill on the floor of her small house. Her grandmother's skin had been a bluish-grey tinge. Severe pain in her stomach made her retch uncontrollably, and the mess had been everywhere. The thought of it made Jennie feel weak.

More warders materialized, scrambling to release the sick, but when Jennie peeked over her scratchy blanket, it was obvious they couldn't keep pace. Up and down the passageway, women and children hung over the edge of their berths, vomiting. Others scuttled down the passageway for the privies, forming a queue that didn't move fast enough.

Jennie wondered how Alice fared, but shrank back, paralyzed at the thought of finding out. Wails of crying, sick children and the moans of the women surrounded her. Jennie's stomach felt light, but otherwise she had no urge to empty its meagre contents. She begged the Lord that she would remain so.

Prisoners thronged to the privies. Nate, his face averted, one hand over his mouth, held a single lantern to show the way. Jennie cowered in her berth tight against the hull.

She heard a rumbling. The heavy wooden hatch door opened. In the dim light Jennie could just make out the second mate's figure partway down the ladder. He held his hand over his nose and mouth, surveying the scene.

"Release all the prisoners!" Meadows sent a couple of the warders to pull out the buckets and mops. "You'll be cleaning up your own mess."

He quickly assigned the guards to seek out those who were well enough to start swabbing and others to assist the ailing. Meadows shouted again. "Let them on deck for air. Half at a time."

As he clomped back up the ladder, Jennie could only imagine what it would be like to escape upwards into fresh sea air.

Scarface appeared at Jennie's berth and climbed up. First he released Flo and Gladys, who both raced for the privies. Hildy descended with care and wobbled behind. As Scarface leaned across the bunk toward Jennie, she cringed. His mouth twisted into a leer as he fumbled to free her wrist from the shackles. She turned her face away from his foul breath as he drew in even closer. What could she do if he attacked her? Should she scream?

"You're a right sweet tart." He squeezed her breast and backed away, grinning.

Jennie's heart thrummed and her palms sweated, as she waited for Scarface to shift to another berth before she moved. She knelt in the other women's vomit as she crawled across the bunk to the edge. She gagged, at last swinging her legs over the side.

As Jennie slid down to the floor, her feet flew out from under her on the slimy straw. She landed on her knees. Grabbing a berth post, she righted herself, just in time to see Sarah heading down the passageway to assist a sick pregnant woman with two small ailing daughters in tow.

Weakly clinging to the edge of the berth, Jennie rubbed her sore wrists and scratched her legs where insects had bitten them. She heard the chaos dimly, becoming lost in a daze behind half-closed eyes. Swallowing hard behind a hand over her nose and mouth, Jennie swayed with the ship's movement. She was thankful the seasickness had spared her so far.

The guards led the first half of the prisoners onto the top deck. Jennie tried to push forward, hoping to be included, but bony hands pulled her back.

"Please," she begged. The reeking confines of the hull were closing in on her. "I must get out."

"So must we all." The hand clamped on her shoulder tightened.

Jennie looked around to find Lizzie glaring at her. Now that she could see her close up, Jennie guessed the dishevelled blonde woman must be older, at least thirty. Lizzie's deep blue eyes were lifeless and wary. She looked frail in a blowsy shift that hung off her skinny, tall frame, but her hands were strong.

"Bide your turn like the rest of us," snapped a pockmarked woman with a haughty, mean look. She had to be Fanny. She was old too, like Lizzie. Her eyes bored into Jennie.

Frantically Jennie looked for another way out. But there was none. Then she caught sight of Alice, immobile on her berth.

"Alice," Jennie called. The young girl didn't stir.

More sharply, Jennie called, "Alice!" Was the child dead?

Jennie climbed up and touched her shoulder. Alice turned her white face slowly toward Jennie.

"Are you ailing?" Jennie asked, relieved.

Tears trickled down Alice's face. "Not in the way you mean," she said. "I just want to go home."

Jennie crawled up beside her as Alice cried quietly.

"We must be brave together," Jennie said.

"Mam always said God never gives a body more than they can bear, but I think He made a mistake this time."

Jennie held her close. "We'll just have to look out for one another then."

"We will?" Alice looked trustingly into Jennie's eyes. "You mean I might be of help to you?"

"Yes. I'm afraid too, and it helps me to talk with you," said Jennie, knowing in her heart that this was true. She also knew that Alice was so much younger, and she must set an example as the older of them, just as she had done for her own sisters. A little ache caught in her throat at the thought of Ann and Beth at home without her.

"I'll be all right now. I'll try to be brave."

"I'm so glad," said Jennie. She gave Alice a reassuring hug and descended once again.

As she returned to her berth section, two women arrived with rags and a bucket to swab the straw mattresses and clean the floors. Jennie moved across the passageway until they were done, grateful she'd escaped the disgusting duty.

From down the passageway, she watched Flo and Gladys support one another as they staggered their way back. Flo's hair hung in damp strings down the sides of her strained face. Her short body wobbled next to Gladys' tall, mannish one.

As they neared, Gladys' legs visibly trembled. She could barely climb up to the top berth again without Flo's assistance. Having first to heave their washed straw pallets onto the other side, so they had somewhere dry to lie, hampered them more.

When Gladys almost fell climbing up, Jennie gave her bottom a shove, then jerked her hands back. She'd never before put her hands on someone's body. When Flo wavered in her ascent, Jennie had no choice but to push her up as well. She felt the woman's bony bottom beneath her dress.

"Pssst." A slovenly, grey-haired woman lying in the next bottom berth motioned to Jennie.

Jennie took a couple of steps toward her.

"Be a luv and bring a swig of brandy for old Dottie, before I takes me last breath." She leaned up on one shaky elbow, staring at Jennie with piercing eyes.

So this was Dottie. Her dress was in rags, twisted around her with a rip down one side from her knee to her ankle. Several of Dottie's front teeth were missing and the rest were black.

Jennie stared at Dottie's alarmingly red face before shaking her head and whispering, "You know there's nowhere to get anything to tipple here."

Dottie yelled, "Bloody listen to your elders! It's me dying wish!"

"You're not dying, only sick." Jennie turned away quickly.

Dottie belched and flung a stream of curses at Jennie.

In her haste to get back to her berth, Jennie almost bumped into Lizzie.

"Make way," Lizzie said. She lurched past to someone's side below her own berth.

Jennie watched Lizzie brush back tendrils of raven-black hair from the woman's flushed face. So Lizzie had a kind streak too.

"How are you Mary *Roberts?*" asked Lizzie.

Jennie heard Mary groan and leaned a little closer to watch the pair.

"I'll waste away to nothin' like some skinny nag. And then where will I be if the toffs aren't attracted to me, and I lose my career?" Feebly, she attempted to tuck her stray hair back into the severe bun drawn tautly off her forehead.

Jennie wondered how the older woman could even think she was attractive. Bags hung under her drooping cow eyes, and her jowls were flabby.

"Don't you worry none, Mary. You won't end up looking skinny as me." Lizzie ran the hem of her dress over her friend's moist forehead. "You'll be up and vexing me in no time."

"Hmmff," said Mary.

"The seasickness will be gone in a few days," Lizzie said quietly and bent over her again. "We'll all be right as rain."

Jennie hoped Lizzie was right.

"How did you become such a know-all?" Mary gave Lizzie a weak puzzled look.

As Jennie leaned a little closer to the pair, she saw sudden dawning light Mary's face.

"You was transported *before*, wasn't you!" she declared.

Lizzie bristled and looked down. "Not exactly *me*, like," she mumbled.

"Used one of them fake names, maybe?" Mary guessed.

Jennie gasped.

Lizzie stood and whirled around to face Jennie.

"You keep your hole shut." She pushed her hands hard against Jennie's shoulders, backing her against the berth so fast that her head snapped back.

Jennie nodded mutely.

"Now, now, Lizzie," Mary said. "You've frightened her enough. She'll keep her tongue where it belongs. 'Sides, what good would knowing do her? That's the past, all over and done with, and where we're going no one cares."

What was Lizzie's name before, and what did she do? Jennie wondered. *More importantly, how did she manage to get home again and back into this predicament?* Jennie decided it would be best to stay out of Lizzie's way, in any case.

She pressed down the passageway through bodies heading back and forth, amid the cloying stench of sickness. She queued to use the privy, but when her turn came, she stared in dismay. Vomit splattered the floor and speckled the walls. The cramped compartment with the narrow filthy board across the front contained only an almost-filled slimy bucket. Jennie lifted her dress and crouched, with one hand over her nose and mouth. But the lack of privacy from the other women and the warders prevented her from relieving herself.

"Pee or get off of the pot, why don't you?" some woman yelled, stamping her feet.

Jennie's face flamed.

"Hang onto your knickers," directed a lilting voice that sounded Irish. "You're only making it harder for the lass. Give her time to do her business."

Jennie peered at the line of waiting women, but she couldn't see who had spoken.

"Be calm," the voice soothed. "Think about something pleasant like when you were a young child snuggling on your mum's lap. Or think about drinking warm milk."

Jennie took a deep breath and let her skirt down a little more over her knees, but not too far, in case the hem dragged in the sopping mess on the floor. She thought about the soothing voice of her mother when she was little, cuddling her and giving her warm milk to drink before tucking her into bed at night.

Jennie's cheeks burned with embarrassment as her bladder emptied, hissing against the side of the pail. Arising and drawing her knickers up in haste, she pushed by the other women in the queue and past the smirking guards, wanting to get as far away from them as possible.

"Wait for me." The calm voice was at her side.

Jennie glanced up and saw a young woman with a smattering of freckles on her face. She had a wide smile with one missing tooth and a head of curly, red hair that bushed out in all directions.

"You're Ir..Irish, aren't you?" stuttered Jennie. She took a step backwards. All her life she'd been told the Irish were no-good, filthy alcoholics and was warned to stay away from them.

"Aye, that I am. Katelyn McDonnell, originally from County Cork," she introduced herself. "I go by Kate. And you must be Jennie, the stealer of stale oats." She gave a little smile.

"You heard?"

Besides being ashamed, Jennie didn't want to get too close to what she had been told were Irish heathens. She wasn't even sure what that meant. Kate didn't seem any dirtier than anyone else, and she certainly hadn't been drinking.

"I have to get some fresh air." Jennie turned away abruptly. She had enough trouble, without being associated with someone Irish.

Jennie saw a swift look of hurt on Kate's face, just before a small, spindly woman hurrying toward the bunks bowled into Jennie. The woman's clothes were smudged and crumpled. The mousey-haired woman talked to herself in a piercing voice. "Da' will be rolling in his grave at what's become of me. The Lord preserve us."

"Iris." Kate kept her voice low. "She's a bit daft a times, but she's harmless – only a right religious nutter."

Jennie frowned. Wasn't Kate a strong Catholic, being Irish

and all? "You speak as if you have turned away from your religious beliefs."

"Well, I certainly don't have anything to recommend God to me," said Kate. She shook her head. "After all the praying I've done over the years, asking Him to keep me and my family from suffering, fat lot of good it did. My Liam is out of work half the time, and the rest of the family is starving. And look where praying has got me! God is certainly not on my side."

Jennie's mind whirled in confusion. Kate's circumstances seemed to be the same as her own. She even felt the same about being let down by God.

Before she could say anything, Kate's voice dropped a notch, and she added, "And being Irish is the worst of it. In the eyes of people like you, we're nothing but trash." Her eyes brimmed with tears and she turned away.

Jennie watched helplessly as Kate skirted around the women swabbing the deck floor. Iris's shrill voice carried over the ripple of nattering and hurried footsteps along the passageway. Jennie's thoughts and emotions clashed, swinging from embarrassment and disbelief to surprise and wonder. What did people think was wrong with the Irish? Kate seemed normal to her, even nicer than most of the women she'd met so far, besides Sarah.

"Move!" Meadows bellowed from partway down the ladder, then disappeared upwards again.

Jennie moved tight against the berths. The women at the bottom of the ladder cleared a path as the first group of convicts descended and filed back to their bunks. Some still retched and lunged for the privies. Once the second group were signalled to proceed, Jennie clambered up the narrow ladder, eager for her first breath of fresh air.

When at last she staggered on deck, she blinked in the bright sunlight. The salty air brought with it a rush of excitement, and she felt light with relief.

Overhead, a seagull gave a piercing call and wheeled off starboard. Water lapped against the hull. The wind whistled through the rigging and the timbers creaked with each roll. Loose strands of Jennie's hair lifted, and the cool breeze caressed her face. Temporary escape from the bowels of the ship felt good. The compression weighing upon her chest eased.

Jennie swivelled around, taking it all in. The sunlight over the water reminded her of a ferry ride across the River Mersey she'd taken with her father one splendid summer day. The sunlight glinting on the water was like an array of sparkling jewels.

"Precious gems for my precious girl," her father had said, laughing and pretending to gather them up for her.

Abruptly, a rough hand grabbed Jennie's arm and swung her about. She found herself face to face with Red Bull, staring into eyes like those of a dead fish. He clamped shackles on both of her ankles. Were they always to be chained, even though the ship was out at sea, and there was no way for them to escape?

There was a sudden burst of wind, and the shipped heaved. A wave of nausea rolled up her throat. She swallowed hard.

"Keep your eyes fixed on the horizon or visible land and you won't be sick." Sarah's welcome figure came up beside her.

Jennie nodded. Standing topside in the fresh air was better than being below, but the feeling of sickness was not so much due to the rising and plunging of the ship. She was sick with terror.

CHAPTER FIVE

WALT APPEARED in front of Jennie. He dragged her midship to the edge of the ship where several crewmen hauled up buckets of water from the sea.

"Hands over the eyes," he ordered. His sullen face registered no emotion.

Jennie couldn't take in what he said. Her ankles throbbed from the chains. Walt grabbed her hand and thwacked it against her forehead.

Suddenly, icy seawater drenched Jennie. She shrieked. Rubbing her stinging eyes only made it worse. Rivulets of water eddied around her feet and over the edge of the deck. Strings of a filthy mop skimmed over her bare toes as a crewman swabbed at the puddles to hurry them along.

"Warned ya'." The wizened-faced warder dipped an old rag into another bucket behind him and thrust it at her.

Gasping, Jennie tested the sodden rag – it had been dunked in fresh water. She wiped the salt water out of her stinging eyes.

"Got another dim-witted one, eh, Walt?" Red Bull smirked as he pushed Jennie into line again behind Hildy and a string of other dripping convicts. Jennie glared at Walt, then at Red Bull.

Her wet dress clung to her, revealing every part of her body.

Her face burned as the crewmen gawked at her, yet she shivered in the cold wind. At least vomit no longer covered her and the others.

On wobbly legs, the chain of women reeled about the perimeter of the weather deck. Sporadically, Jennie grabbed onto the railing. They circled several times before Jennie was able to walk more steadily. On they tramped, past the cargo boom and the capstan, avoiding ropes, iron posts, hooks and leering sailors, past the jolly boat and longboat stored at the stern. Behind her, Sarah whispered encouragement as they followed the grooves worn in the planks. The continual beat of a drum kept them in step.

The warders were quick with their clubs if anyone lurched too far out of line. None did on purpose, but the pitching of the ship left many scrambling to stay upright and some had to stop and heave their stomach contents overboard.

Above, the tall sails whipped in the changing wind. An occasional seabird gave a sharp cry. Whinging pulleys and ropes on one of the sails being heaved in added to the cacophony of sounds. Jennie rejoiced at her first taste of freedom from the black hole below. Gradually her shift dried and her body warmed, even though the sky had turned cloudy.

Halfway up the line, Jennie spied Alice. The little girl looked peaked, and the chains were too heavy for her slight body as she staggered to keep up with the drumbeats. Jennie vowed to take Alice under her wing whenever she could.

Kate was ahead of Alice, with her red curls blowing into her face. In front of her was Fanny, the doxy – whatever that was. Jennie vowed again, this time to keep her distance from Fanny and Lizzie. And for now, Kate too. She'd stay near Sarah. She felt drawn to her, maybe because she reminded her a little of her grandmother. Sarah puzzled Jennie, though. She spoke like she'd had some education, but that didn't suit what Jennie imagined of a chimney sweep's wife.

Jennie ventured in a low voice over her shoulder, "Have you had some schooling, Sarah, if you don't think it rude, my asking?"

"No, I've had naught," the woman whispered.

"But your speech isn't like, that is, you speak real well," Jennie twisted back to look at the woman. "And you seem to know so much."

"I don't speak like a chimney sweep's wife, is what you mean?" Sarah gave her a hint of a smile.

Jennie blushed. The assumptions she'd been making about people were all topsy-turvy now.

"No need to worry about offending me. My own dear mum worked as housekeeper in a titled master's house, and I'd often go with her. That's where I learned to keep my ears and eyes open. I paid attention while the children were being schooled."

"Shut your yaps!" Scarface cracked his whip over their heads.

Jennie clamped her mouth shut and stared straight ahead. Out of the corner of her eye, she felt the eyes of Red Bull roaming over her body. She didn't like to think about what he planned to do if she ever stepped out of line.

Terrified, she scanned the bedraggled women and the rough crewmen and warders. Everything was so foreign to her, and there was no one who could help her. She thought again of what Alice's mother had said. *God never gives us more than we can handle*, but those words of wisdom didn't comfort her any more than they had Alice. It was clear that Alice's mum hadn't been in such circumstances as the two of them were now.

She flashed back to her own mother's earnest face, moments after the coppers showed up at their door to snatch Jennie away to jail.

"God go with you and give you strength to make your burden light. May He see fit to bring you back to us one day." Her mother had hugged her fiercely, whispering into her ear. "Hold onto your faith, and know I'll love you always, wherever you go." Her mother had tried to press a locket into her hand, but one of the coppers stopped her.

As they rounded the stern, Jennie glanced up at the tall masts piercing the overcast sky. The sails billowed tautly in the wind. A huge wave of emptiness and longing washed over Jennie. She might never see her family again.

"We've no recourse now," sighed Sarah, once they were a safe distance down the deck from most of the guards. "Look there."

There was no sign of a coastline in any direction; only the never-ending, grey sea mirrored by the dreary mackerel sky. The desolate sounds of the wind, the water and the odd call of a seabird emphasized Jennie's isolation.

"We mustn't be far from shore if there are still birds," she murmured. She watched several brown and black and white birds criss-crossing the wake in search of scraps.

"Far enough," Hildy chortled in front of her. "It's a long swim back."

Jennie jerked her head around.

"Some birds will fly two days out," Hildy continued.

"Stop your blathering," a young guard blustered from the shadows of the wheelhouse.

When they drew even with him, Jennie was surprised to see it was Nate. He was younger than she'd originally thought. Up close, his face was smooth except for a few fine chin hairs. His hazel eyes solemn, he pretended not to notice Jennie, but finally looked away as she found herself unable to stop staring at him.

Jennie wondered why such a young man was a guard on a harsh convict ship. He looked like someone more suited for the land. She glanced over the sailors at their various stations. Several of them were young too. Straightening, she plodded on in silence, except for the clanking of her leg-irons.

All at once, a woman's agonized scream rent the air.

Wide-eyed, Jennie strained to see around the others popping their heads out of line to look toward the stern.

Another high-pitched scream reached them.

Whispers scurried up and down the line. Whips cracked.

"Order!" bellowed the harsh voice of First Lieutenant Yates.

Jennie straightened in line with the other women.

"Eyes forward!" The harsh voice roared over yet another scream.

Jennie went rigid with fear as she neared the wheelhouse. A shrieking woman with her arms stretched above her head was manacled to the end wall. Red Bull flogged her, obviously finding pleasure with each stroke. The woman's dress was in tatters to her waist and her body jerked with every lash of the whip. Her bony back bled, the flesh covered with welts and long, open slashes.

When Red Bull stopped momentarily, the woman's screams subsided into agonized whimpers and cries for help. Stunned, Jennie could hardly take it all in. How had she not noticed the flogging frame before, or the punishment balls and torture irons strapped to the wheelhouse?

"Oh, no, not the black gag," Hildy said.

Bile rose in Jennie's throat as Red Bull stuffed the wooden bit of a leather bridle into the woman's mouth. Buckling the straps around her head and neck, he snatched up the whip again. He lashed at her, grinning at his audience. The woman's body bucked, though her legs were slack.

Ahead of Jennie, Alice howled and began sobbing.

"Shut the brat up!" Scarface yelled.

"Hush, hush, hush," Kate begged from behind the girl.

"Look away, Alice," Sarah called out.

The flogging continued for several more beats of the same

drum to which Jennie and the other convicts marched around the deck. Jennie glanced over and away again, cringing with each crack of the whip. The leather thongs ripped at the woman's back. Her body jerked, but otherwise she appeared lifeless.

At last Red Bull stopped. He removed the gag and the manacles. The woman slumped heavily to the deck floor. As two other warders plucked up the unconscious woman by her feet and arms, her head lolled to the side.

Lizzie.

The other doxy! All the air left Jennie's chest. Why Lizzie? What had she done to cause such a flogging? Had they discovered her other felonies, her other name? But surely that couldn't matter.

"Let that be a lesson to anyone else who disobeys orders or plans to mutiny!" Red Bull barked, as the two warders hauled Lizzie's limp body down the open hatch.

Jennie gasped. Lizzie disobeying orders? Planning a mutiny? That made no sense. She'd had no time.

"Let's be thankful they didn't put her in the coffin bath." Hildy indicated a long, low rectangular box.

"What's it for?" Jennie murmured, not sure she wanted to know the answer.

"Soaking a lashed prisoner in sea water." Hildy's response was barely audible.

"With open wounds?" Jennie remembered how the sea water had stung her yes. "How horribly cruel," she managed to sputter.

"Probably saving the coffin for later in our journey," whispered Gladys.

"Aye, for now they've set a terrible enough example to keep us in line for a long while." Sarah's voice trembled.

Hot tears ran down Jennie's face.

Alice sobbed anew, and Jennie was glad someone was there to console her, even if it was Kate.

"Hold your tongues!"

Jennie could barely breathe as they continued their rounds. She couldn't shut away the image of Lizzie's torn back.

When the ship's bell rang to mark the end of the half hour of fresh air, Jennie didn't know whether to be relieved or sick. Her thoughts flickered over the jolly and long boats tethered at the far end of the ship, but escape was out of the question – especially now that she knew the consequences for a failed attempt. Besides, where would she escape to? She had no idea how far they were from any coastline. And if by some slim chance the opportunity ever did arise, she'd have to be incredibly certain of succeeding.

Meadows ordered them back down the hatchway, and Red Bull removed their leg irons once again. When Jennie reached him, he yanked the restraints off her ankles, scraping them on purpose. Jennie held back a cry of pain.

Sneering, he whispered in his heavy Yorkshire accent, "You'll be next fer whippin' if you don't do 'xactly what I tells you to." He peered down her cleavage.

She shrank away from him. He was a worse menace than Scarface.

Below deck, more of the condemned were suffering from seasickness. The guards thankfully left the prisoners free of their wrist manacles. But the brutal whipping had subdued everyone, including all the young children, as they trotted in silence back and forth from berths to buckets.

As Jennie passed the surgery, she glimpsed Lizzie lying, comatose, on a cot inside. There was no sound from her. Jennie stumbled to her berth, tears coursing down her cheeks. She wanted so desperately to go home! She was barely able to see as she climbed into her bunk.

If only that freak accident had not killed her father! His career as a chaise maker was safe compared to jobs in the mines or at the mills. Only the horrible chance of his being underneath the heavy front of a carriage at the exact moment it slipped off its blocks had robbed her family of a decent life. One second of terrible timing had crushed him and left them impoverished. Much later, another second of bad timing on Jennie's part had brought her here. Why had she taken the oats just as Mrs. Burgess threw out the slops? It had left her family even more destitute, had left her suffering in these horrible conditions.

She sobbed harder.

"Shh, shh," Sarah said from somewhere below her. "We'll be all right."

Alice called out in a frightened voice, "Jennie whatever can I do to help you? Please tell me."

A sob of a different kind caught in Jennie's throat. She pressed her hand to her mouth, trying to gain control.

"Are you in pain? Shall I shout for the surgeon?" asked Alice.

After a few moments, Jennie answered Alice in a muffled voice, "I'm just frightened."

"Would it help if I sang to you?" Alice asked. "That's what my mum does when I'm afraid."

Jennie's eyes welled with tears again. How sweet of Alice to comfort her. It was almost like having one of her sisters nearby. Jennie let out another stifled sob. Alice and Sarah were all she had now. They were her new family.

"I think singing would be a fine thing for you to do, Alice," said Sarah.

"Aye, let the lass sing. Cheer us all up, it will," said Kate.

"Go ahead, luv," Sarah said.

In a clear, confident voice, Alice sang:

Twinkle, twinkle little star
How I wonder what you are
Up above the world so high
Like a diamond in the sky

When the blazing sun is gone
When he nothing shines upon
Then you show your little light
Twinkle, twinkle all the night

Then the traveller in the dark
Thanks you for your tiny spark
He could not see which way to go
If you did not twinkle so.

In the dark blue sky you keep
And often through my curtains peep
For you never shut your eye,
'til the sun is in the sky.

As your bright and tiny spark
Lights the traveller in the dark
Though I know not what you are,
Twinkle, twinkle, little star.

"Well done," said Sarah, clapping along with several of the women.

"Thank you, Alice." Jennie dabbed away her tears.

"Do you know another?" asked Flo.

The girl said, "I learned one at the big house where they sometimes had parties, and people sang." She paused. "But maybe it's too sad for us."

"Let's hear it anyway," said Hildy.

"Yes, you have such a lovely voice," said Kate.

Alice began the first verse:

Mid pleasures and palaces though we may roam,
Be it ever so humble, there's no place like home;
A charm from the sky seems to hallow us there,
Which, seek thro' the world, is ne'er met with elsewhere.
Home, home, sweet, sweet home,
There's no place like home,
There's no place like home.

When Alice reached the second verse, stumbling slightly over the words, Jennie joined in quietly, along with a few other voices, including Sarah's. Hildy and Flo hummed. Gladys sang aloud. Iris's high-pitched, off-key voice quavered above everyone else's when Alice started the third verse. Jennie and her bunkmates sang the words strongly and several young children joined in the chorus.

By the last verse, it seemed like everyone was singing – except for the warders, though they didn't complain.

As the last chorus died away, more than a few people were sniffling. Many praised Alice, clapping their hands together or rapping on the wood of their berths with their knuckles. Jennie swiped at her tears and dried her hands on her shift.

From the guardroom, someone hollered, "Shut those women up."

The young warder heading in their direction called in a subdued way, "That's enough now!"

As Nate passed Jennie's berth with the lantern held high in front of him, she thought she saw a glisten at the corner of his eye.

Though a kind of quiet had reigned for a brief time, the privies were still in constant use with women and children rushing down the passageways in both directions. Jennie's berthmates left, sometimes to be sick and other times to visit someone needing help.

After one such time, Sarah, weary and pale, collapsed into her berth.

Jennie crawled over to the edge of her bunk.

"Can I help?" she asked, dreading the thought of what that might entail.

"Nothing you can do," Sarah moaned, clutching her stomach and drawing her knees to her chest. "You are fortunate, Jennie, not to be so afflicted."

"'Tis not the movement of the sea that ails me," Jennie agreed. Indeed, it was the confinement in the hulk of the ship with no way out that troubled her.

"You! Get down here and grab a mop."

Jennie jumped at the sudden appearance of Scarface. "Me?" she asked.

"Who else is lollin' about and gabbin', while others are ill?" Scarface snarled. Jennie cringed away as he laughed and tried brushing down her chest.

Jennie awkwardly descended, and she slipped on the slimy floor. The stench rose up. She stared at the mess around her in a daze.

Scarface thrust a mop at her.

"You seen a mop and pail before?" he asked, sarcastically. "Move it, or you'll be another to get a floggin' for insubordination." He stomped away.

Jennie made a feeble attempt at cleaning a spot, but suddenly felt light-headed. At once she turned her thoughts to her father. What would he have done if he were in her place? But then, he probably never would have been someplace like this.

Her father, besides possessing fine carpentry skills and a reputation for hard honest work and fair dealings, had been well-known beyond their immediate community. She felt a swell of pride. Word of William Lawrence's talents had even reached the ears of royalty. He was awarded a commission to build a special royal carriage. He took Jennie with him to deliver it, and that included a ferry ride. Her father, a descendant of the honoured Lawrence family, who fought so valiantly in the Napoleonic Wars, had never shirked his duty. Surely, Jennie could show some of that Lawrence bravery now.

She drew back her shoulders and gave the mop another few wipes across the timber flooring. As she bent to wring out the foul mess, she suddenly went light-headed again, and her body sagged. How was she going to endure these abhorrent conditions for the next four months? Would she ever safely see land again? And if she did, what horrible fate awaited her? Could it be worse than the conditions on board the ship?

Booted footsteps of a guard stomped toward her. Jennie knew Scarface was coming back. She grabbed the mop and pushed it vigorously across the floor. The footsteps faded as she worked her way toward the surgery.

She glanced inside. Dr. Weymss was dabbing up the blood from Lizzie's open wounds. Once he seemed satisfied that the bleeding had stopped, he smeared what looked like lard from a pail onto them and started to wind strips of cloth around her body.

Jennie shuddered. Lizzie's back was a horrible ribboned mess of ragged flesh. The surgeon wasn't even taking time to suture them so that her cuts would heal flat and smooth.

Without thinking, Jennie blurted, "Aren't you going to stitch the wounds first?"

The surgeon turned to her in surprise. "What does it matter?"

"She'll be horribly scarred if you don't," Jennie said.

"She'll most likely be dead before she reaches our destination anyway, with the attitude she has. Besides, it takes too long."

Sarah wobbled up behind Jennie on her way back from the privy. "You could help him. You have skills with the needle."

Jennie gaped at Sarah. She'd only sewn gloves and dainty women's collars and underthings. How would she ever be able to sew flesh?

"If you had some help to sew her wounds, would you take it?" Sarah asked Dr. Weymss.

The surgeon shrugged.

"You can do it." Sarah gave Jennie a little nudge. "Same as sewing gloves."

Jennie stared at Sarah. Using needle and thread on gloves was totally different.

Lizzie made a pitiful sound, though she still seemed unconscious.

Sudden resolve swelled through Jennie. Never was it more important than now that she show her Lawrence fortitude. She set aside the mop with no regret.

"I'll help sew her wounds, Dr. Weymss, if you show me how."

CHAPTER SIX

CLANG! CLANG! BANG!

Jennie cracked her eyes open and squinted in the gloom.

"Five-thirty a.m. Rouse yourselves!" This time it was Walt's footsteps stamping along the passageway, yelling and clanging his club against the bunks. Annoyed mumblings and rustlings sounded up and down the length of the berths.

"Get up, you layabouts!"

Jennie inched her sweaty body away from Hildy and mopped at her face. The humid confines hadn't yet dried from the constant swabbing of berths and floors. Nor were they likely to for quite some time. Vaguely she recalled a constant shuffling of people moving along the passageway all night, still plagued with sickness.

Though her other injuries were starting to heal, Jennie's arms ached from the gruesome task of stitching Lizzie's back. Once he'd seen her handiwork, Dr. Weymss had left her alone to labour for hours.

Lizzie had lain unconscious through most of it. She moaned in relief only as Jennie smeared soothing lard on her wounds when she finished sewing the ugly ripped skin. Lizzie's back would still be heavily scarred, but at least there wouldn't be such deep gouges. That is, if she lived. Jennie wasn't sure how anyone could survive the severe flogging Lizzie had endured.

Lizzie! Did she make it through the night?

Bleary-eyed, Jennie crawled over her bunkmates and slid down to the floor. As she started toward the surgery, she scratched at the bedbug bites all over her body.

"Take your mattresses and hammocks deck side with you."

The order came from someone standing in the shadows at the bottom of the hatch. "Those of you on this side first." Nate stepped out of the gloom and pointed to Jennie's group. He stared as if straight through her.

Jennie felt her face redden as she turned back to retrieve her bedding, and then she stumbled awkwardly along with her companions, carrying their rolled sleeping gear. She paused to peer into the surgery, and someone nudged her forward. But she'd managed to catch a glimpse inside. Lizzie seemed to be breathing. Otherwise, it didn't look like she'd moved since Jennie had tended to her. The white strips of cloth binding her wounds were blood-pink in places. Had some stitches let go? Jennie wanted to go to Lizzie, but dared not leave the line of women. Red Bull's threat for disobeying orders was too strong in her mind, and the evidence of doing so was right before her eyes.

Jennie handed her mattress through the hatch to a relay of upper deck crew and then climbed up. Emerging topside into the subdued daylight, she glimpsed a sailor lashing the mattresses to the gangway nettings for storage.

"You'll gather them again at the end of the day." Meadows' orders caught her attention. "Now, line up in front of Surgeon Weymss."

She watched as the surgeon doled out something in a teaspoon to each of them.

"What's that?" asked Jennie.

"Lemon juice – daily ration," Nate said in passing without

looking at her.

"Wouldn't want us gettin' scurvy and dyin' on them," Hildy whispered.

Jennie looked at Hildy in alarm.

Beside her Sarah nodded. "One more thing to worry about in this hellhole."

Jennie drew a deep breath and waited for her turn.

Overhead, a smattering of gloomy clouds hung low in the sky. The birds had disappeared. The wind held the tall sails taut in the stiff breeze. The water slapped against the ship as it sliced through the waves.

"Wash yourselves and get back below deck," Meadows ordered, once Jennie and some of the others had swallowed the sour juice.

Unsteadily, Jennie followed the others to a line of buckets, each three quarters full, sitting on the right side deck floor. The water sloshed from side to side with the movement of the ship.

She glanced at the row of warders, standing behind them with smirks on their faces, Red Bull among them. Closing her eyes, Jennie scooped water onto her face. She gasped. Cold sea water again. Her insect bites stung. At least she was half expecting it.

Behind her, the guards chuckled.

There was no way she would wash any more of herself. She stepped away from the bucket.

Red Bull growled in her ear. "Finish!" He gave her a shove.

Jennie bent and cupped a little water into her hand. She held her breath as she scrubbed at her neck.

"Faster," Red Bull snarled.

Bracing herself, she splashed water onto her arms, underarms and the top of her chest.

Suddenly, the red-bearded monster grabbed the bucket and sloshed the water over her. It dribbled down her body, and the salt stung her bites and scrapes. Jennie struggled to catch her breath. Red Bull ran his hands over her shoulders. She wrenched away from him. He pulled another woman into her place.

Grabbing a damp rag near the bucket, she tried to mop herself dry. Sarah handed her a tatty hairbrush after she finished brushing Alice's hair. Jennie tugged through the tangled wet ends of her own hair, before passing it to Hildy.

Avoiding Red Bull's leers, she stared at the cold, grey sea and the endless dull sky. Everywhere there was water and more water, sky and more sky, grey upon grey and the ever-present smell of the sea.

A crack on her shoulder brought her to stark attention. Rough hands shoved her into line with the other women. In a daze, Jennie took a last breath of salty sea air, and ducked down the hold.

Below deck, Jennie was surprised to see that the other half of the prisoners had positioned plank tables and benches underneath where the hammocks had hung. Some were in front of the surgery. With the door closed, there was no way to enter undetected to check on Lizzie. A few women squabbled about where they were going to sit, but were quickly brought to order by the guards, who shoved them onto the benches. Jennie managed to seat herself between Sarah and Alice, who gave her a weak smile. Jennie patted Alice's hand, as a shrill whistle sounded. Meadows called for their attention.

"Each table will choose a captain of the mess. That person will be responsible for the good order and cleanliness of their mess and for distributing the rations to their tables. They will see that the women at their assigned messes wash themselves every morning and sit together as you are now. The mess captain will also make sure each of their members takes turns cleaning the utensils, which will now be doled out to you." The crisp voice ordered the utensils brought forward from the galley.

A young boy lugged out a pail of spoons, counted them out and clanged them down on each table of twelve for the women to distribute. The clattering of passing them around almost drowned out the whispering and loud grumbling around Jennie, as each table debated who would be the captain of each mess. No one seemed to want to be responsible for imposing the strict warders' rules on the others.

"Enough!" yelled Meadows. "Each of you at the aft end of the table will be the mess captain." At the bewildered expression on most women's faces as they looked from one to the other, he pointed in the direction he meant.

"No bloody way I want to be responsible for the lot of you," Flo complained, realizing she was designated.

Still grumbling, Flo went with the other mess captains to serve breakfast from more buckets handed to them by the cook's crew. She slopped thin gruel into the wooden bowls. Jennie rose to help distribute them.

"I don't need no help," Flo grumbled.

"Let her," said Hildy. "We're hungry, and you're too slow."

When she sat down to eat, Jennie dipped her spoon into the pale slime. It was no better or worse than what they'd had in prison, though Jennie thought it might be slightly more watery, and, after tasting it, not salted enough. Yet, she ate ravenously, her stomach clamouring for more, but it was not forthcoming. In fact, the last ones served got even smaller rations than those at the start.

"Bloody pigs," said Dottie, one of the ones shorted at another table. "Serve me first next time, you dolt," she said, waving a menacing finger at Hildy.

"I'll wash the utensils," Alice offered, carefully gathering the spoons and bowls from those seated at their table.

"Good girl," said Jennie.

Alice flashed her a grateful smile. Although several spoons

clattered to the deck floor as she headed for the ladder, Hildy helped Alice retrieve them.

"She's smart too," said Sarah, nodding approval. "Be first and get it over with."

Jennie wondered where the utensils were being cleaned. She hoped it wasn't in the same swill pails where all the women had washed.

"Inspection time. Everyone on deck, except those assigned to stay below," Meadows ordered.

"Reverend Ernest Brantford will lead you in prayers." The reverend had combed a few strands of his grey hair over his balding head. Clasping a Bible with his long bony fingers, he began his ascent.

Jennie trundled up top again with the others. A handful of women, including Kate, were told to stay put.

"What's happening below?" Jennie asked.

Hildy answered. "Probably inspecting our quarters for contraband. You know, in case we've smuggled spirits or knives or something on board since we left the docks."

"As if we had a chance!" Flo rolled her eyes.

Fanny guffawed. "Maybe they are looking for the lice and bedbugs." She scratched at her neck.

"No," Sarah chided. "I hear they are to clean the hold, and the surgeon is inspecting to make sure they do it the way he wants."

"He'd do better to get rid of the bloody bugs," said Fanny.

"Quiet, please," Reverend Brantford's firm, low voice commanded. He led them in a prayer filled with the fear of damnation for all their sinful ways.

Jennie winced with each scolding. Alice clutched her hand in fear.

"Kneel, you sinners," he said, "and repent!"

As Jennie and the others fell to their knees, she noticed Fanny and Mary Roberts only partially crouching with smirks on their faces. Most of the women looked bored, though a few had bowed heads. Behind Jennie, Iris sobbed and prayed aloud.

At last, the reverend reached the end, and a loud chorus of "Amen" echoed around Jennie.

"Half of you will exercise now, and the rest will go down to do scripture readings and learn your letters and sums," Reverend Brantford said. "Those on starboard, follow me below."

Jennie started forward, but many women had no idea which side they were on and collided. Jennie still remembered the parts of a ship her father had taught her on the ferry ride.

"No, no. Not you, and not you. Yes, you," said Reverend Brantford impatiently, as the guards helped him organize the women and line up those staying on deck behind Jennie.

As she waited for the women to get sorted, Jennie noticed Fanny saunter with hips swaying behind the wheelhouse. Almost immediately, Red Bull disappeared after her.

"Now march, you lot," the reverend ordered Jennie's group. "The rest of you follow me."

As they filed past the wheelhouse, Jennie craned her neck, searching for Fanny. Her eyes almost popped out of their sockets at the sight of Fanny with the front of her dress up around her waist and Red Bull's lower body pressed tight against her, his breeches hanging loose partway down his backside.

Jennie gasped.

"Look away," hissed Sarah from behind her.

Jennie shielded Alice's eyes, hoping the girl, who was ahead of her, had not seen anything.

"Are we playing a game?" asked Alice.

Jennie let out a breath of relief, dropping her hands as they passed beyond view.

"Yes, you have to guess who's behind you," Jennie said wildly.

"But that's silly," said Alice. "I already know you're behind me."

"You're right, pet," said Sarah. "Jennie is just larking about."

"I expect you wanted to take my mind off things," said Alice, flashing a grateful look back at Jennie. "But I'm fine now. Really."

Her eyes were so serious and sad, Jennie wanted to hug the girl and whisk her away to somewhere safe. "I'm glad to hear it," she said.

Sarah patted Jennie's shoulder and whispered, "Well done."

Jennie felt shaken. Now she thought she understood what they were talking about, what a doxy was. A horrible flush of mortification rushed through her body. Was this what she would be forced to do for the rest of her life?

"Agh," she yelped, as the young warder poked his club into her side.

"Move along, you," Nate ordered.

"The name's not *you*. It's Jennie Lawrence," she said, in a sudden flash of anger.

His eyebrows lifted in surprise. "Uh, Nate Pickering. Now, move along, uh miss...Jennie." He indicated that she needed to catch up with the others.

Jennie joined the line of women, wondering where Nate was from. At least he could be somewhat polite. She suspected he might even be a pleasant sort to chat with, if they weren't in these circumstances. But they were, and he was her guard, and he irritated her. She concentrated on walking mindless circles to the monotonous drumbeat. How far was it around the deck? How many miles would they walk before the ship arrived at their destination? How many drumbeats would they have to hear?

As she circled the deck, Jennie was vaguely aware of the sailors darting to and fro, working with the sails. Meadows directed them with sharp commands from the bridge. When the ship's bell rang, he shouted, "Coombs, your turn for dog watch."

"Aye, aye, sir." A fair-haired man sprinted to the mainmast.

Jennie watched one agile sailor scramble down from the crow's nest. "All calm ahead," he reported as he passed Coombs.

"Thanks, Edwards," Coombs replied. He clambered up the rigging like a spider on a web racing toward freshly caught prey.

Jennie shook her head. She and the other women were all prey on the ship with no way to escape their cruel predators and the endless monotony of their ordeal. All she could do was plod on and pray she'd escape from the worst of their circumstances. Other than working in the surgery, she needed to keep a low profile.

There were no guards at the base of the ladder on the return trip down to the ship's bowels, and Jennie managed to slip into the surgery. The only light came from an open porthole. It was enough to see that Lizzie was sleeping, though fitfully. Gently, Jennie examined the red-stained bandages. They needed changing, she was sure, but how long would it be before she was missed, if she stayed to do it?

Jennie lit a small candle lamp and hung it on the hook above the table where Lizzie lay. She gently removed the soiled bandages, one by one. Mopping at the wounds, she cleaned them as best she could, and then smeared on more lard, before placing clean strips of cloth over them.

She was surveying her handiwork when suddenly, the door opened. Jennie jumped. *Dr. Weymss!*

He gave her a stern look and inspected her work without a word.

At last, he grunted, "You may go."

Jennie made for the door.

"You will be one of my assistants for the rest of the journey," he added. "You and Kate and one of the Marys."

Jennie looked back at him, but he had busied himself at another table. She thought about Kate being one of the surgeon's helpers. If the doctor asked her to work with him, maybe she wasn't so bad after all. Jennie slid out the door, closing it gently behind her, and joined the others who were studying their letters at the mess table.

Within moments Jennie was pressing hard with her chalk, trying to copy what Reverend Brantford had given them to practise.

"You seem to be getting the hang of these squiggles," said Sarah, obviously perplexed. "These mawleys of mine are too stiff now." She wiggled her stubby fingers in the air. "I doubt I'll ever be able to do it as fine as you."

Jennie looked up at her friend across the table. "I want to write a letter home and send it as soon as we land. I want my family to know where I am."

"And just how will you pay for the paper and Penny Black postage, Miss Prim?" asked Fanny, leaning over her left arm to inspect Jennie's work.

"I'll worry about that later," Jennie answered. She'd forgotten about the new postage system that had been put in place a couple of years earlier. She had no idea where she'd earn a penny to afford the stamp.

"Perhaps you'd like to do favours for the sailors?" Fanny taunted.

"What kind of...?" Jennie broke off, suddenly recalling Fanny locked with Red Bull on deck.

Fanny gave her a sly wink. "Not the kind you'd be wanting to do, I'd bet."

Jennie was sure even the roots of her hair had turned red with embarrassment. Somehow, she'd find a way to post the letter, or else find someone who would take it for her. What she didn't know was if, or when, the letter might reach her family. Jennie bent back over her work.

She wanted to finish copying the alphabet again before they had to go for another trot around deck or stop for their pitiful dinner. She could tell by the smell wafting toward them that they were having pea soup – probably watery. She'd heard that occasionally, if they were lucky, lumpy plum pudding or maybe some sort of unidentifiable gristly meat might appear, though the rations would never be enough to stave off hunger.

Beside her, Alice did her best to follow the marks the reverend had assigned them. She did quite well, though slowly, her one elbow on the table, or resting her head in her hand. She looked so sad. Jennie glanced around. Reverend Brantford loomed over a table on the other side of the area.

"Alice, are you ailing?" Jennie whispered, wondering what she could to do lift Alice's spirits.

"Missing my mum." Alice's voice was so soft Jennie almost didn't hear her.

"I miss mine too," said Jennie. Her mind flashed to what they must be doing without her.

"I didn't do anything wrong, and I didn't even get to tell her," said Alice.

"Would it help if you talked about it?" asked Sarah kindly.

Alice nodded and leaned closer to Jennie.

"For stealing, Jennie, but I never. Truly I didn't," whispered Alice. "They just thought I did."

Slowly Alice revealed how her mother, who was an undercook in an aristocratic home, brought her in as a kitchen helper after her father and brothers had been killed in a collapsed mine.

"It was ever so much hard work, scrubbing those big pots and hauling out the slops. That's when it happened like, when I hauled slops. I found the mistress's hair comb in the yard. I put it in my pocket to return it to her. Only I forgot right away like, as Cook had me hauling cauldrons about all day."

"And you're such a wee thing too, to be doing such heavy work," said Kate.

"Well, and...well," Alice continued, "Cook wanted to get rid of me so her sister could work in the big house."

"What happened then, pet?" asked Sarah gently.

"It was only at night I remembered. I took it out of my pocket and laid it on the floor by my bed pallet. I was going to return it in the morning. Only Cook saw it when she came in to scold me for missing a pot. She called me a thieving brat and hauled me before the housekeeper. Cook made sure the housekeeper and the mistress of the house didn't believe me. They let me mum go too; they said 'cause she hadn't raised me proper like. I don't know where she is now." Alice began sobbing softly.

Jennie put an arm around her and hugged her close, keeping an eye on the reverend's movements.

Everyone at the table went silent for a few moments.

"You've been such a brave girl," Sarah said. "Your mother will be proud of you wherever she is."

"Thank you," Alice said. She sat up straight, rubbed hard at her eyes and wiped her face as the reverend headed in their direction.

Jennie winked at her, and Alice nodded with a little smile.

The bell clanged for mealtime.

After they ate their allotted dry biscuit, there was another stint on deck to facilitate the sweeping of their quarters, each half of the convicts taking turns. Then it was Jennie's group's turn to attend scripture lessons.

Reverend Brantford droned through most of his lecture, until he came to a passage that particularly spoke to his strong hopes for their salvation. His passion unleashed, he fairly screamed at them, the stray lock of grey hair bouncing into his eyes with each fervent point. Jennie half expected the man to fall to the floor in a dead faint from his exertion.

"Beg for forgiveness for your felonious behaviour!" he implored, pointing his long, bony fingers at them each in turn. "Or God's wrath shall rain down on you, and you shall suffer hellfire and damnation, forever and ever."

Jennie quaked inside, her mind in a turmoil. She hadn't known she was such a terrible person and still didn't understand why God would rather they starve than feed themselves as best they could. She was so very sorry she'd taken the oats, but what were they to have done instead? Especially as the sack had been in the rubbish bin. She'd seen too many of her neighbours waste away from lack of food. Why did God want her punished so severely?

Behind her, Iris intoned, "Yes, yes, the Lord has something much better in store for us. He has a grand purpose and we shall know it soon."

Jennie had a sinking feeling that God had forgotten them altogether.

CHAPTER SEVEN

WHEN THE WARDERS extinguished the lights at 8:00 p.m., Jennie feared it would be another sleepless night of fending off bedbugs. From the moment she landed on her pallet, she'd begun swatting at them.

"Bloody nippers!" Hildy wiggled beside her.

"I thought the sun and sea air was supposed to get rid of them," said Gladys, slapping her body.

"Maybe from the mattresses, but that doesn't help if they're not gotten rid of down here in the hold," Flo said.

Others complained too, but they had little recourse. Jennie faintly heard the whispered grumbling as fatigue overcame her.

The next thing she knew, flames consumed her. Licking at her from every direction, bright orange and hot. She screamed.

Hildy gave her a swat. "Wake up! Quit your screaming!"

Breathing heavily, Jennie was relieved that she'd only dreamt of being in hellfire. The fear the reverend infused about eternal separation from her loved ones shook Jennie to her very core. Obviously, all her praying so far was not enough. She'd have to do more. She mumbled the Lord's Prayer, she made up prayers, she begged for her soul and forgiveness for her sins in loud whispers.

"Quiet!" Hildy swatted her again.

From then on, Jennie said the prayers in her mind, begging for mercy.

As THE DAYS and nights passed, Jennie dreaded dusk, when she and her cohorts hauled their bedding back down to the hold again. Inevitably, she endured the almost sleepless nights fending off vermin and nightmares.

Although sick at heart, Jennie was thankful that she'd withstood any serious bouts of illness. Seasickness continued to affect many of the women for the first week and a disease of the bowels attacked almost all of them into the second.

Dr. Weymss finally solved the problem by dispensing a compound of sulphur of magnesium to each of them, followed by doses of castor oil and some other tincture that tasted like chalk. Jennie hated the taste, but didn't want to be sick. Their routine and the management of the ship appalled Jennie and varied little, as did their atrocious food, which she knew was the reason the women were ill.

Oft times they were served tiny portions of salted meat for supper, which barely filled a little corner of their stomachs. Jennie had trouble nibbling the hardtack that went with it, having to smack it on the edge of the table to break off a piece. What was worse, as time went on, the heat below deck was almost suffocating and the stench unbearable.

Their cramped quarters filled with the odour of the bilge below them, where the ship's animal wastes were stored in gravel that was impossible to clean. The stink of vomit was the hardest to take, next only to the fetidness of the sick and dying women and children. Some had been ill even before the voyage began, and they didn't last long under the harsh ship conditions.

The prayers, commencing again on the main deck afterwards, left little to be thankful for, so Jennie stopped praying altogether. Except for the threat of eternal flames, could hell be very different from life on this ship?

Jennie was happy to escape the drudgery of routine by occasionally helping the surgeon suture cuts whenever accidents befell crew or convicts. Kate was there too, whenever an extra pair of hands was needed. Of any of the Marys, there was no sign.

"Have you ventured to do nursing before?" Jennie asked Kate timidly one day.

Kate laughed. "Not at all, though I do have a little experience with a saw."

Jennie looked at her in puzzlement.

In her lilting voice, Kate explained. "I got hauled up, unjust like, for cutting someone's shrubbery. It hung in front of our doorstep for an age. My Liam's back was acting up something dreadful. After a full shift of work, he had to crawl through the bloody stuff to get into the house."

Just at that moment Gladys came by on her way back from the privy and poked her head in. She had overheard and said, "Neighbours can have bloody cheek all right, Kate, can't they?" She stepped into the surgery.

"Those neighbours were just plain mean," said Kate with a sniff. "They didn't even eat the plums off the branches. Just let 'em rot. So what if we helped ourselves to a few while we cut back the branches?"

As Jennie listened in amazement, Gladys commiserated with Kate and then blurted, "Mine had me nicked for feeding me family a chicken." She went on indignantly. "We was hungry and it was strutting about free like, not in any pen. I ask you, how was I to know it belonged to our neighbour and that it wasn't free for the taking? Chickens all look alike."

"That's right, Gladys, as if you could tell." Kate gave a hoot of laughter, and they grinned at one another. Jennie smiled sadly at the injustice of all of their plights. They really did seem to be very much alike – for certain in the eyes of the law.

"What's all the gabbing about?" Sarah stepped in to join them.

While Gladys and Kate filled Sarah in, Jennie recalled other similar stories she'd heard from her former cellmates while awaiting punishment. She was saddened most by the injustice of transporting convicts for the minor crimes. The lowest sentence for transportation was seven years for even the most trivial misdeeds. Everyone she knew from her old neighbourhood was starving, and if they hadn't stolen yet, they were on the brink of doing so, or perishing.

Gladys echoed Jennie's thoughts when she spoke. "What's a body to do when you are famished with no means to make a living?"

"Aye," Sarah responded. "Is the government going to see everyone starve to death or jailed and shipped off to other countries? Sir Robert Peel may have made some good reforms, but there are some he should have left alone, or some he should yet make, like feeding the poor."

"There won't be anyone left in the country soon," said Gladys.

"Except the rich," Kate said.

"Can you picture the toffs carrying out their own slops?" Gladys snorted.

"Shh," Jennie said suddenly. Was that the guards? Or had Lizzie stirred? She shooed the others out of the surgery. But there was no movement from Lizzie, who still lay unconscious.

Over the next few days, Jennie continued to check on Lizzie, changing her dressings as needed. Surgeon Weymss told the warders to give Jennie free access to the surgery to care for her patient.

When she wasn't helping Alice with her letters, Jennie escaped to the surgery as often as she could, puzzling over the various tins and jars filled with powders, dried plants and liquids. The sight of them reminded her a little of her grandmother's scullery, and that calmed her somewhat. She studied the labels until she could read them, but didn't know their purpose unless Doctor Weymss happened to use them. Then she secretly watched how he applied them and for what illness.

She also kept Lizzie company, though Lizzie never acknowledged her. At first, Lizzie slept a great deal, and at every slight movement she twinged with pain and whimpered. After the surgeon left each day, Jennie chattered to Lizzie about her home and family when her father was alive, even though Lizzie never responded.

One afternoon, as she straightened and dusted the medicine containers, Jennie prattled about the wonderful flower gardens they used to have; how she and her sisters, when they were little, chased butterflies and hid in the tall grass at its edges.

"Stop your nattering," Lizzie croaked. "I can't listen to any more about your cheery home life."

Jennie was so surprised at Lizzie's sudden outburst that she didn't take offence.

"You've recovering!" she said, rushing to Lizzie's side.

"Yeah, and the sooner I can get out of here and away from you the better," Lizzie grunted.

Jennie beamed at her.

Lizzie turned her head away, but not before Jennie saw a tear slide down her cheek.

The next time Jennie returned, and for several days afterwards, Lizzie was sullen, but more vocal. She expressed her discomfort at every spasm of pain, as Jennie removed her bandages and cleaned her wounds. When Jennie spread salve on her wounds, Lizzie said nothing, though Jennie knew Lizzie felt soothed – her features softened.

"Where you'd learn to nurse, in a butcher shop?" Lizzie carped one day.

"I don't know how to nurse at all." Jennie laughed.

"Your hands are cold," Lizzie continued to grouse with a slight smile on her face.

"That's because your body is so hot. It's working hard to heal you."

Lizzie grunted.

"Why did they beat you?" asked Jennie lightly, smoothing salve onto Lizzie's right shoulder.

"What did they tell you?"

"Disobeying orders and planning a mutiny. I know that last can't be right," said Jennie.

Lizzie cursed. "Mutiny! If I'd been planning a mutiny, I would have succeeded, and I sure wouldn't be bone-headed enough to let them find out."

"Why did they say that then?"

Lizzie let out a stream of oaths, and mumbled about horrible things she'd like to do to the man with the red beard.

"You mean the guard who flogged you? Red Bull? What about him?" asked Jennie.

"He lies," said Lizzie and that's all she would say on the matter.

Ten days after her beating, Lizzie managed to sit up for a bit, though in dreadful pain. That was the same night Dottie was brought in suffering from dysentery. Jennie tried to tend to her too, but the doctor didn't give much hope for Dottie's recovery.

One evening a few days later, Dr. Weymss deemed Lizzie ready to go back to her own berth.

"I'll get her settled in," Jennie said to the surgeon.

"Fine, but she'll be expected to take part in all the exercises and work, so there's no point in mollycoddling her." The surgeon turned on his heels and headed for the ladder.

"But she can barely walk," Jennie protested.

"All the more reason she manages to do things under her own steam soon." The surgeon spoke from halfway up the ladder without turning to her. "The guards will pick on her like a sick chicken and won't thank you for coming to her aid."

"But she needs time to heal." Jennie's protests fell on deaf ears.

"Leave it," whispered Lizzie. "It's part of the punishment. I'll be fine." She swayed to her feet, and waved Jennie away when she tried to assist.

Weakly Lizzie lurched down the passageway, pausing to lean against posts and berths. Jennie walked next to her, ready to catch her if she fell. All was well, until Lizzie reached her berth. She gasped with each movement as she stretched up her arms and tried to climb.

"Don't. You'll rip open your stitches," Jennie protested.

"I've no choice."

"Yes, you do," Kate's lilting voice came from the bottom bunk where Sarah also lay. "I'll trade with you. You take my place down here."

"I don't want that heathen doxy near me," objected Iris from next to Kate.

"Some kind of Christian you are then, not to help another human being. You're just a mean-spirited old woman," Sarah said with a sharpness in her voice that Jennie had never heard before.

While Jennie was surprised by Sarah's rough manner, she also noted Sarah's acceptance of Kate, and Kate's kind offer. Perhaps the things that Jennie had been led to believe about the Irish weren't true.

"Don't put her right next to me," Iris squealed again.

"Push to the back then, because she's staying," said Sarah. "We'll all shift so Lizzie can have the front. It will be easier for her."

"But not for us," grumbled Iris as she squirmed against the hull. "Lord help me to persevere." She began a fervent mumbled prayer.

Barely had the space been made, when Lizzie slumped half on and half off the bunk.

"She's fainted," gasped Jennie. "Shall I get the surgeon or a guard?"

"A guard will be too rough. The surgeon won't come. We'll manage," said Sarah. She and Jennie eased Lizzie's top half onto the bunk. Kate climbed out and lifted Lizzie's legs.

Once they had her settled, Jennie tended to Lizzie's back, making sure the stitches held and the bandages were in place. Satisfied, Jennie climbed slowly to her own berth and collapsed.

The daily routines passed in an endless blur for Jennie. She didn't know how much time had elapsed, nor did she care. Sometimes she felt numb, and at other times, she had to quell the fear that seized her and made her as helpless as a rabbit in the jaws of a fox – especially at night.

Although Jennie frequently awakened from sleep, scratching at lice and bedbugs, or in terror from her nightmares of burning in hellfire, once it was the whisper of warders creeping past her bunk that woke her. Dottie had expired in the surgery one evening at 8 p.m. as the roll call before bed was underway. The surgeon hadn't been able to do anything for the elderly woman's dysentery-ridden body. Even though she'd never liked Dottie, Jennie thought it was a relief that she hadn't had to suffer any longer.

When Jennie heard the creak of the infirmary door, she knew that's where the warders had gone. A short time later, she heard the light rumble of the ladder being put in place and then some thumping and whispered cursing, followed by a scuffing sound.

Jennie peered through a narrow slit in the berth boards, but darkness shrouded the guards. There was a tap, and someone from above opened the hatch door a crack. A faint light from overhead revealed three figures, struggling with what looked like a bulky body wrapped in a blanket. It took some time before they managed to manoeuvre their load onto the deck and close the hatch again.

Several moments later, Jennie heard a distant splash. Had they just dumped Dottie into the ocean? No one had been able to say good-bye, and no prayers had been said over Dottie! She was just gone. True, the surgeon was afraid others might catch her illness, but surely Reverend Brantford could have had some kind of prayers for her before they dumped her so unceremoniously into a watery grave.

Jennie recalled others that had died and some who'd gone mysteriously missing. She wondered now if they too, had been heaved overboard in the middle of the night as fodder for the sharks. She'd never thought before about what happened when people expired on the ship. Had no one else been awakened tonight? Were they all oblivious?

She heard the hatch creak open again, and saw the warders return with an empty blanket in their arms. They stowed it back in the infirmary. Unmoving, Jennie stared into the dark, as they rustled past her. The guardroom door hardly made a sound as they opened it and slipped inside.

After that the ship seemed to settle back into its familiar gentle creaking, as if breathing a sigh of relief. It was some hours, though, before Jennie fell into an uneasy sleep amid the usual snoring and muttering.

And then she dreamt of hands reaching for her, pulling at her. She flailed out to keep them from heaving her into the sea too. "Don't throw me overboard!" she cried out.

Smack!

Jennie jerked awake, her arms punching wildly in the air, her heart pounding.

Hildy smacked her again. "Hit me one more time, and I'll pulverize you," she hissed.

Jennie dropped her arms, staring wide-eyed into the dark.

"Lie still, or Dottie won't be the only one to leave the ship tonight. I'll dump you overboard myself." Hildy flopped her head away.

So, others *had* heard. She hadn't been alone in what she'd witnessed. Somehow, knowing that did little to calm Jennie's anxiety. Sleep came no more to her that night.

CHAPTER EIGHT

THE NEXT MORNING, Jennie attempted to ask about Dottie, but tight-lipped warders ignored her. She waited until Alice had gone to clean the utensils after breakfast before whispering to the others at her table about what she'd observed in the night.

"That's eleven dead so far," said Hildy. She sported the beginning of a bruise around her left eye. "Was almost one more." She rubbed her arm and gave Jennie a fierce look.

Jennie hadn't known that many women had died.

"They'll put it down to them being sick before they boarded," Flo replied. "They don't care if we live or die."

Sarah tried to reassure them. "Those days are supposed to be gone. That's why they've hired surgeons on ships now," she said. "Dr. Weymss' sole responsibility is for our well-being."

Although this was of little consolation, Jennie hoped it was true.

Fanny guffawed. "That's only because the captain receives a bonus to land us safe and sound at the end of the voyage."

"And that's only for the ones they say weren't sick before we sailed. You can bet they lied about the number of those too," said Hildy.

Was it true what they said? Jennie looked around the table.

What if most of them didn't make it? Who would care?

"But there are too many dying now. Surely, the authorities must know there weren't that many sick before they left," Sarah said.

Flo snorted. "Too late for the ones that are already gone, ain't it!"

"Yeah, and what're the authorities going to do about it once we get there? Can't bloody well resurrect the dead," Fanny spat out.

"The doctor would be in for it too, if he let us *all* get sickly and die," Sarah added.

"He's probably in cahoots with the captain."

"I'm sure he had to hand over some kind of records before we left port. No point in getting het up about it," said Sarah in a calm voice. "They can't let us all die," she repeated.

"Too bad they weren't a little more concerned to begin with," said Fanny. "If they don't start feeding us better, we'll all be fish food, whether they have a doctor or not."

"At least the surgeon tastes our meals now to make sure they are cooked proper," said Sarah.

"We still could get scurvy and all of us die like what happened in them earlier ships," Hildy countered.

"That's why they give us lemon juice," Sarah argued. "Though I admit it doesn't taste the freshest."

"Soon they'll have to give it to us in the rum to keep it from going off completely," said Lizzie, not looking like that would be altogether a bad thing.

"Too bad someone doesn't do something about the way they treat us too. You call that swill they give us as water, fit for washing in?" whined Flo.

"And what about keeping us packed down here like cooked sardines," said Hildy. "This heat can't be good for a body."

Hildy indicated Lizzie, sitting quietly at the corner of their table, her hair tangled, grime on her face. Lizzie hardly spoke to anyone any more. During meals she rocked with her arms drawn over her chest rather than eating. Sometimes Jennie made attempts to feed her by placing pieces of biscuit in her hand and guiding it to her mouth. Otherwise, she might not have eaten at all.

"They keep this place like a pigsty and treat us no better than pigs," agreed Flo.

"The pigs are probably treated better." Hildy scowled.

"Geez, listen to you," said Fanny from across the way. "You're still thinking you're on a voyage to somewhere exotic. We're prisoners, for Christ's sake."

"Do not take the Lord's name in vain," Iris scolded. Her high voice rose an octave as she continued to admonish them.

The hurled insults continued, but Jennie's thoughts crowded them out. She did her best to keep herself as clean as she could with the small amounts of grimy water they had to use. She, like many of the others, moved about with an arm or the collar of her dress pressed to her mouth and nose while below deck, but the lack of oxygen and stifling heat made her dizzy.

Jennie's favourite time was on deck during a fair day, savouring the brisk air and sunlight. She took full advantage when parading around the deck for exercise, stretching and strengthening her aching muscles, as much as the confines of their parading lines would allow. The spray of waves refreshed her, especially now that all of her wounds had healed.

Fanny complained whenever Jennie sped up, enjoying the bracing air on deck.

"Quit messing us up, Miss Prim," she'd heckle and try to pull Jennie back into a regular pace.

At those times, Jennie took in deep breaths of salty sea air, and made believe that her stomach didn't ache continually, that her hair wasn't matted and that her clothing wasn't smelly and threadbare. She almost persuaded herself that marching to the beat of the drum around and around the ship meant she *was* heading to an exotic life somewhere. She found it hard, though, to pretend she didn't miss her family and her home horribly, and that her pale and haggard shipmates were not an indication of how she looked too.

The warders had removed leg irons and chains on deck totally after the first couple of days away from land, easing their movements slightly. They were marched in a continuous line, three deep. Jennie kept to the outside of the deck, so she could concentrate on the changing colours of the water – from blue to grey to black and every shade in between. She soon became familiar with the moods of the sea.

One day it was calm and smooth as if sleeping, and the next it would angrily knock them about. Sometimes the sea would frolic and splash and roll happily. Those times made it hard to walk, but Jennie's spirits always lifted, as did the boredom of sedately walking.

But eventually even a playful sea failed to rouse her. One dreadful day after another passed, punctuated only by the mood of sea and weather. They were never close enough to any land for birds to appear. At times, it didn't seem to matter if it were light or dark, night or day; time simply unfolded all around her, and Jennie had no awareness of it.

"Not feeling so chipper today, Miss Prim?" Fanny asked one particularly sombre morning.

Jennie said nothing as she stared at the bleakness of the sky blending into the dismal grey of the water. The vast, endless sea and sky melded with the void she felt inside. It was as if she didn't exist.

Without realizing it, Jennie had stopped walking. But a sharp whack on her shoulder brought her back to the bleak present. Walt loomed over her, his wooden club ready to strike again, if she dared talk back or dallied any longer.

"Does it please you to strike me?" she asked without thinking. The prisoners around her stopped.

Walt stood, speechless for a moment, before he stammered, "Only doing me job!"

"How would you like it if I hit you?" she challenged.

His face flushed, and he gave her a forceful shove. "Move on!"

From across the deck, Jennie saw Red Bull watching the exchange. When she came abreast of him, the huge, muscular man roughly grabbed her arm.

"Actin' up again, you tart," he mocked. "We'll see about sortin' you out once an' fer all."

He flung her aft of the mainmast partially out of sight of the others, and gave her a thwack across the shoulders. She tried to leave, but he grabbed her, letting his club drop. He pinned her against the wall with the full weight of his body.

She tried to scream, but he clamped his big hand over her mouth, and yanked up her dress.

She bit his hand. Hard. He cursed.

"Let me go," she managed to cry out before he slapped her and jammed his hand back over her mouth.

The harder she squirmed, the more his eyes gleamed with excitement. Suddenly, Jennie let herself go slack.

"That's more like it." Red Bull pawed at her clothes, groping at her bodice.

With a sudden jerk, she rammed her knee into his groin, and then shoved his chest hard.

He flew back with a painful gasp and doubled over. She ran from his clutches.

The other guards who had gathered around laughed. Red Bull groaned and made a clumsy lunge at her. He grabbed her ankle and she fell, face down. Wrenching her over, he plunged his body full length on top of her and jammed the side of his hand into her mouth. With his other hand, he ripped at her dress and fumbled at his breeches.

Jennie tried kneeing him again, but he was too heavy, and her legs were pinned. She bucked and twisted beneath him, trying to get away from his rough hands. He banged her head against the deck, and she lost consciousness for a second.

All at once, Nate was there.

"I've had enough of you hurting these women!" he yelled and grabbed Red Beard's arm. "Let her go!"

Red Beard swung at Nate, but didn't connect. "You're a dead man," he spat. "Both of you are as good as dead," he added, jerking his head at Jennie.

"Enough sport," called Captain Furlee, stepping out of his cabin, though he had a smirk on his face.

Nate jerked Jennie away and helped her to her feet. Her chest heaved with unreleased sobs.

Suddenly Lizzie lunged from out of nowhere, wielding Red Bull's dropped club. With a mighty swing, she aimed at Red Bull's back. He noticed her and turned his head just as she whacked him hard. The blow fell across his face.

Jennie heard a crunch of bone and saw a spurt of blood.

Lizzie kept swinging, hot with rage.

Red Bull blindly scuttled away from Lizzie, holding his nose and mouth.

Yates ordered Meadows and Scarface to go to Red Bull's aid and others to subdue Lizzie. Lizzie kept swinging wildly at the guards until they brought her down. They restrained her arms and legs and hauled her away kicking and screaming.

Nate looked on with horror. His face suffused with anger, he moved as if to help Lizzie. Captain Furlee commanded him to restore order with the women. Nate whirled away, pushing the women back into line. He left a couple of them to gather Jennie into their fold.

She sobbed aloud then, clutching at her torn dress, trying to hide her shame. Sarah hurried over and helped adjust her clothing. Mending was the only thing that would help repair much of her dress. Head down, Jennie walked as quickly as she could to the stern, barely aware of Kate helping to shield her. Bruises were already forming on Jennie's arms, and she hurt all over. She couldn't stop shaking.

"Stay near me from now on." Sarah's grandmotherly comfort calmed her.

"I'll watch out for you too," Kate added.

Jennie nodded, as Fanny sauntered over to join them.

"You're all right – for a tart," laughed Fanny, who must have overheard Red Bull's remark.

"I'm not like you," Jennie retorted. She clutched her torn garment tighter to her chest with both hands.

"Maybe not, but you're still feisty! I like that," Fanny clapped her on the back. "Come on, Miss Prim, loosen up. It was a joke."

"I don't think you're funny at all," Jennie fumed, jabbing out to shove Fanny.

Fanny sidestepped Jennie and ducked around Sarah. "I think she's out of the shock phase; what do you think?"

Sarah nodded. Jennie crumpled into herself and sobbed.

Sarah and Kate supported her on either side as they circled the deck on their rounds. Fanny strutted behind, her manner defying anyone to tangle with any of them. Jennie looked for Alice, but was relieved to see that the girl must be below deck, taking her turn at sweeping the hulk.

When she was somewhat calmer, Jennie asked, "What will happen to Lizzie now?"

"The same as before, I –" Fanny started to speak, but Sarah cut her off with a shake of her head.

"Please – not another lashing." Agitation gripped Jennie. "She won't survive!"

"Almost certainly a jail cell for the rest of the voyage," said Sarah.

"Oi," Fanny agreed.

"After all, the guard attacked you," said Sarah.

"But that's the point. He attacked *me*," said Jennie. "Now Lizzie's in trouble because of helping *me*."

"What's done is done. There's nothing we can do to reverse the clock," said Sarah.

"But why did Lizzie try to save me?" Jennie asked.

"Maybe because you saved her," said Kate.

"But I didn't," Jennie said.

"You helped heal her," said Sarah.

Kate added, "I suspect she wanted to thank you for your kindness in stitching her up."

"But what good has it done if they whip her again?" Jennie asked.

Fanny stopped and turned to Jennie. "Make no mistake, she also did it to get back at the guards for what they did to her," she said. "Whatever happens to Lizzie is by her own doing."

"We'll do what we can to help her, wherever and whenever possible," said Sarah.

A wave of knowing seemed to pass through the four of them. Jennie realized there had been some sort of bond formed, and even more, she'd joined some unspoken code of the criminal element to protect one another.

Jennie put her hands on her hips. "That will be the problem...wherever and whatever we can do will be too little. That's not bloody much good, is it?"

Sarah looked at Jennie in surprise.

"Yes, I swore, and I'll bloody well do it again," said Jennie. She stamped her foot. "I'm so tired of being ordered around on this vile shite-hole they call a ship."

The look of surprise on the women's faces stopped her.

Suddenly Jennie sank against Sarah's shoulder. Tremors racked her body, but Sarah held her tight, until she'd gathered her wits about her again, Kate and Fanny urging them to move forward.

As Jennie righted herself, a dark cloud passed overhead. She shivered.

Crack! Crack!

A horrible scream ripped through the air.

"Take that you bloody bee-hitch." Red Bull hollered.

Jennie stopped in her tracks. All strength drained out of her. Sarah stared at her, white-faced and still.

"That's enough," shouted Captain Furlee. "She'll not live."

"And you can't afford that," Fanny hissed under her breath, clenching her fists. "Bloody vicious bastards!"

"No!" Jennie screamed and ran toward the sounds of Lizzie moaning.

"Jennie, wait!" Fanny called after her.

Red Bull pushed Jennie savagely out of the way. She caught herself from falling. Captain Furlee ordered Scarface and Walt to untie Lizzie and haul her back to the hold. Lizzie's back was split open again. The captain didn't stop Jennie, as she plunged down after them. Behind her, she heard the guards barring the others from joining her.

She pushed her way into the surgery where they'd laid Lizzie on her stomach. Jennie covered her own torn dress with a surgeon's apron. She was already mopping at the blood from Lizzie's raw wounds when Surgeon Weymss appeared at her side.

"Bloody stupid woman," he muttered, looking Lizzie over. "She has a death wish. I'll not waste any more of my time on the likes of her."

"You can't abandon her," said Jennie aghast.

"I can and I will. Do what you want. You'll do just as well as me. She probably won't live this time." He grabbed a bag, threw some bandages and a small splint into it and stomped out of the surgery. "I have a guard with a broken nose to tend to."

Though upset at the surgeon's dismissal of Lizzie, Jennie set to work, thankful that Red Bull wasn't being treated in the surgery with them.

Lizzie became more cognizant of her surroundings, as Jennie cleaned and stitched the gaping wounds. Re-stitching over partially healed ridges was more difficult than before. Jennie flinched as she jabbed the needle into sore skin, but there was no way she could make it any easier on Lizzie, who swore under her breath each time.

"Sorry," said Jennie.

"For what?" Lizzie said, sucking in her breath. "Your fancy sewing saved me once."

"Well, I'm getting tired of doing it!" Jennie said more sharply than she intended. "Why did get yourself flogged again?"

Lizzie went quiet, but Jennie wanted answers. "What is it with you and Red Bull?"

"Not that it's any of your business, but that vile piece of filth is a lying bastard." Lizzie cried out in pain as Jennie came to a more tender area.

"So you said before. What about? If you tell me, maybe I can help. Like speak up for you to the captain."

Lizzie snorted. "Not that easy, Miss Prim. So that's all you get."

No matter how much Jennie urged, Lizzie wouldn't say anything more.

Even after a few days when she was a little stronger and transferred to a jail cell at the back, Lizzie still refused to tell Jennie or anyone else more about her situation.

Jennie made a concerted effort to keep her distance from Red Bull. Fanny kept an eye out too, and she, Kate and Sarah hurried Jennie along any time Red Bull appeared in her vicinity. His broken nose healed crookedly and some of his teeth were missing, but Jennie felt no sympathy for him. Luckily, the surgeon had not called her to help suture his face.

SEVERAL MORE WEEKS into their voyage, Jennie's spirits flagged even more than they had before. The food, never enough to begin with, began to run out, and the hardtack rations became smaller, staler and harder, tasting of mould and leaving her with no appetite. Her body weakened, and she was often too tired to do more than drag herself around the deck. She discovered that numbing her mind to a careful blank became easier and easier to do – no thoughts, no memories, no appeals. And no thought of prayers either.

"Buck up," Fanny said to her one day. "If you don't keep our spirits up, who will?"

"What's the use?" Jennie mumbled.

"We'll have fresh food soon," Sarah said. "We should be reaching Tenerife any time now to take on fresh supplies."

"Never heard of it," Fanny said.

"The island belongs to Spain, though 'tis off the coast of Africa." Sarah smiled when Jennie raised an eyebrow in wonderment that she knew this. "I heard the captain tell one of his men."

"An exotic destination after all," said Jennie. "Though not quite the kind Fanny meant."

The others kept silent.

If only she could figure out a way to escape from the ship when it pulled into port, maybe she'd somehow find safety. Her thoughts flickered over the jolly boat and longboat, but she quickly dismissed the idea. Even if she could get past the guards and crew that surrounded them, there was no way she would get far with the armed soldiers on the poop deck leaning over the railing above them. She daren't express her thoughts to anyone else. She alone must be responsible for the consequences for any plan that might fail. But then she realized, she didn't know how to row, hadn't a clue what direction to take and besides, there was no food. She'd never survive alone. But surely there must be some way of escaping from this hellhole. For the moment, she couldn't think of one, but something would come to her. It had to.

CHAPTER NINE

As THE DAYS PASSED, the weather became sullen and blustery for long stretches, and Jennie brooded, alternately dismissing one futile escape plan after another. Her moodiness increased as rain kept them trapped, ciphering and learning sums down in the hold for days on end. Brief forays on deck, though cold and repetitive, kept her from going crazy. Watching Coombs and Edwards and the other sailors gave her something to do. She wondered how they could stand the monotonous work in the numbing cold, wet weather.

Even Reverend Brantford's rants lacked fervour. His words had become meaningless to Jennie, and she ignored him. As well, memories of her family and worry about them faded as she went through the motions of existing day after day.

Jennie sometimes slipped down to the jail cells to check on Lizzie. The warders gave Jennie passage to go most anywhere, respecting her ability to help the surgeon. Moreover, she'd sewn up some of them. Scarface had caught his hand in a winch, almost ripping a finger off, and Red Bull had slashed Walt's neck with a knife in a drunken brawl.

Jennie had tentatively tended to the warders, leery of their hot breaths and lewd remarks, as she'd worked on their wounds. She feared they'd lash out if her ministering hurt them more, but most tried not to show their pain. Nate appeared one day, his face bloody, but he refused to say a word, only wincing as she cleaned him up and applied salve to his wounds.

The ugly bruises on Lizzie's face and body from the blows she received after attacking Red Bull were fading. The welts on her back, though still healing, left unsightly ridges despite Jennie's careful stitching. Jennie hoped they looked better than they would have if she had not intervened.

One stormy evening, Jennie found Lizzie shivering in a corner of the jail cell, curled up as tight as a shrivelled leaf. Most of the inmates languished against the bars, the hull and interior walls. Some lay on a scattering of straw pallets stretched out on the floor. Many slumbered and snored to the pitching of the ship and the moaning of the timbers. Wrist chains secured others in place.

Among them was Crazy Mary Hilling, rocking on her heels and banging her head against the hull. She nattered in a demented way with an occasional screech, her eyes glassy and distant. Sometimes Jennie wondered if she would end up like Crazy Mary. Now and again, her mind played tricks about where she was. On more than one occasion, Jennie discovered she talked to herself, not to one of her sisters as she'd imagined.

She cleared her head and reached through the bars to rouse Lizzie. Her arm was hot! Jennie shook Lizzie gently at first, then harder until she opened bleary eyes.

"Come closer," Jennie whispered. She didn't want Crazy Mary to hear and start caterwauling. "You have a fever. Let me look at your back."

Lizzie weakly shifted toward Jennie and slumped near the edge of the cell.

Jennie peeled back a bandage, and Lizzie moaned. A couple of the deeper gouges were angry red and swollen with pus.

"You have wounds that aren't healing properly," she said. "I'll be back."

Jennie headed to the surgery, but when she pounded on the door, Dr. Weymss wasn't there. What medicine did Lizzie need?

A warder stood in the shadows at the bottom of the hatch ladder.

"Can you get the surgeon for me?" she asked.

"What's ailing you?" he asked, stepping out of the gloom.

Jennie's heart sank. It was Walt. Good luck with him doing anything to help, but she tried anyway.

"Not me. It's Lizzie," she said firmly, hoping he wouldn't see her quaking.

Walt snarled. "He's not likely to come for that hellcat."

"Please, you have to get Dr. Weymss."

"Is it an emergency?"

"Yes!"

He snorted. "Unless that vermin's dying this minute, I'm not fetching him."

"She *will* die, if she doesn't get some attention right away."

"Pah! It would be good riddance to bad rubbish."

Another warder came up from the passage behind her. Jennie turned to find Nate staring at her. Concern flitted across his face.

"Please, can you get the surgeon for Lizzie? She's really ill."

Nate looked uncertain.

Jennie pleaded with her eyes.

Nate turned to Walt. "Where *is* Superintendent Surgeon Weymss?"

"Having a chat with Captain Furlee. If you disturb them to help that doxy tigress, it's on your head."

"If she doesn't get help, she'll surely die." Jennie pleaded with Nate.

She turned back to Walt. "You don't want another dead

convict, do you? How will the authorities take that at journey's end? No bonus for your captain and probably not for you."

Walt shrugged his shoulders and turned away. She looked to Nate again.

He pressed his lips together, seeming to have made up his mind, and scuttled up the ladder.

Jennie slipped into the surgery as Walt wandered away down the passageway. She scanned the labelled bottles on the low table, trying to figure out what would be best to use. She picked up a bottle and tried to make out the label.

"Away from there!" Dr. Weymss yelled from the doorway. "Do you want to poison her?"

Jenny jumped. "No, I want to heal her. Her wounds are festering. So tell me what's needed."

"Saucy, aren't you?" The surgeon raised his eyebrows.

Jennie faced him defiantly.

"Fine, if you want to learn more than stitchery, then watch carefully."

As she stepped closer, she caught a whiff of rum on the surgeon's breath. He'd been doing more than chatting with the captain.

Dr. Weymss selected a jar containing some dried, white flowers.

Jennie strained to make out the label.

"Achillea millefolium," he said, without turning to look at her. "Yarrow."

He measured a little into a small mortar dish and ground it up. Into the powder, he spilled a few dried orange flowers from a tin and crunched them up too. "*Tagetes* – marigold."

Jennie's mother had grown marigolds in her flowerbeds, and yarrow grew wild in the nearby fields when they lived in the cottage before her father died.

"I didn't know flowers were good to make medicines."

"They will suffice in this case because we don't have any maggots to suck out the pus."

Jennie grimaced, sure that if they looked around the ship they could have found some. But she wasn't going to suggest it. She wouldn't be able to put slimy fly larvae into Lizzie's wounds.

"And that?" she asked, as Dr. Weymss poured a clear liquid from an amber bottle.

"Fish oil." He added, "We're out of linseed oil." He stirred it into the dried flower concoction.

"And that's it?" she asked, as he set the containers back onto the table.

"And lard of course." He reached for a bucket, added a small lump of lard and stirred the mixture into a creamy paste.

"You'll need to apply the liniment on the infected areas just as you've done before."

"Me! Aren't you going to look at her?"

He shook his head. "You are quite competent to go down there and do it yourself."

Jennie's mouth dropped. "Aren't we bringing Lizzie here?"

"No. Captain's orders. She might attack the warders again."

"But she can barely move."

"All the more reason to leave her where she is." He shoved the salve at Jennie, along with some cloth strips. "Slather it liberally."

"Can you at least get the guards to open the jail cell?" Jennie asked.

"No. There are too many dodgy convicts to control." He grunted. "Some are too dangerous for the likes of you."

He followed Jennie out the surgery door, shut it firmly and climbed the ladder, muttering in annoyance. "Disturbing me for the sake of a woman who's going to die soon anyway."

Incensed, Jennie made her way down the hushed passageway. Although there was no more seasickness, lethargy and weakness had set upon most of the convicts. They stayed in their bunks when they didn't have to do chores or their daily routines, so she met no one in the passageway, not even children playing pick-up sticks with slivers of planking. As she passed Sarah's berth, the grandmotherly woman asked if she could help.

"I'll manage. Thanks." Jennie patted Sarah's arm. "There really isn't much room to move back there."

The jailed women were mostly asleep when Jennie returned, and Lizzie hadn't moved.

Jennie shook Lizzie gently through the bars to awaken her. "Can you move your back a little closer to me?"

Lizzie opened her glassy eyes partway, and shifted a little, but collapsed.

A light hand touched Jennie's shoulder. She looked up.

"I can help." Alice squeezed next to her and knelt on the floor.

Jennie nodded, and again peeled the cloth from one of Lizzie's wounds. Lizzie whimpered.

"It needs to be lanced and drained," said Alice.

Jennie looked at her in surprise.

Fanny pressed in beside them. "And how do you come to know that, wise Alice?"

"A mouser cat at the big house got infection from a dog bite on its back, and that's what had to be done," said Alice. "We need something pointy like a knife and some hot water."

"But how can we ever get those things?" asked Jennie. "The surgeon won't be bothered, and the warders won't help."

Fanny whirled away without a sound and tapped on the guardroom door.

Red Bull yanked the door open. "Whaddya want?" His expression changed from anger to pleasure when he saw Fanny.

Jennie bent her head back down and watched Fanny from the corner of her eye.

Fanny swung her hips, and, brushing her body against Red Bull's, she whispered something in his ear.

Running her fingers down his chest, she said aloud, "I can make it worth your while."

"Hold this for me, please, Alice." Jennie shoved the bucket of salve toward the girl.

The door squeaked closed, and Fanny was gone.

"Perhaps we could squeeze the wound open to drain it," Jennie suggested.

Alice shrugged. "It might work."

As Jennie took up a piece of cloth, Alice set the salve on the floor and stroked Lizzie's arm. She sang quietly. Jennie pinched a small swollen area.

Lizzie shrieked.

"Sorry," Jennie said. She sat back on her heels and fretted over the angry red wounds. What to do next?

Crazy Mary began shrieking and banged her head against the hull in the cell.

"I don't think it would hurt as much if we could use a knife," Alice said, wiping Lizzie's perspiring face with the hem of her dress.

All at once, the door behind them opened and Fanny emerged from the guard's quarters. Her clothes were rumpled and her hair mussed, but she had an air of triumph about her. She held out a gruel-sized bowl of steaming water. When the door closed behind her, Fanny pulled out a penny knife from the folds of her dress.

"He gave you a knife?" asked Jennie.

"Not exactly," said Fanny slyly.

Jennie gave Fanny a grateful smile, though her heart felt heavy. She knew what Fanny had done to get the items that would save Lizzie.

Alice took the small folding knife. Carefully she poked the

sharp tip along a tiny edge of a festered wound. Lizzie didn't seem to notice.

Jennie tried to keep herself from gagging at the putrid smell.

While Alice continued to pierce the infected wounds, Jennie mopped away the pus. Fanny handed her strips of cloth dunked in hot water. Jennie cleaned and soaked the wounds with the hot compresses; then she and Alice applied the salve. Fanny piled up the pus-soaked cloths, along with the soiled bandages. Jennie was amazed at how well the three of them worked together, cleaning and rebandaging Lizzie's back.

When they were done, Lizzie looked up with grateful eyes, before slumping into delirium. She mumbled something about blackmail and getting back at Red Bull.

Jennie turned to Fanny with a questioning look.

Fanny shook her head. "Don't know what she's rambling on about."

"Maybe it has something to do with Red Bull being a convict too," said Alice.

Jennie and Fanny stared at the young girl.

"I heard Lizzie telling him she knew about his crimes." Alice looked at them in all innocence. "One day ages ago, when we were on deck."

"Out of the mouth of babes," said Fanny. With a little chuckle, she moved closer to Alice.

Jennie smiled. "Did you hear what crimes?"

Alice shrugged. "Not about that."

"What *did* you hear?" asked Fanny.

"Nothing that made sense. Just talked about some old codger. Bailey, I think they called him. Old Bailey."

Fanny mouthed something at Jennie. Jennie nodded. It had to be the courthouse in London. Intrigued, Jennie quizzed Alice. "Did it sound like they knew each other before being on this ship?"

"It was hard to tell."

"Did they mention any other names?"

Alice shrugged again. "Not really. Other than Red Bull called her Maggie, and Lizzie kept insisting that was her sister's name."

"That's it?" asked Fanny.

"Yes, other than something about Red Bull owing her money."

Fanny and Jennie exchanged glances as Alice knelt back down to smooth the mixture remaining in the bucket.

"Will we have to put on more salve later?" Alice asked.

"Indeed we will," said Jennie. "Would you like to help later as well? You've done a fine job here."

Alice looked pleased.

"We'll come back before bedding down time," said Fanny, kneeling down to straighten Lizzie's crumpled dress over her bandages.

"See you then. I'm going to Sarah now." Alice scurried away.

"So, maybe Red Bull is a convict too," murmured Jennie.

Fanny agreed. "There's probably lots more to that story."

"Do you know her sister Maggie?" Jennie asked.

Fanny shook her head. "She only has a half-brother that I know of."

"Then who's Maggie?" Jennie asked.

"Not a sniff," said Fanny, shrugging. She picked up the knife, made a small slit at the bottom of her dress and slid it into the hem.

Jennie hardly noticed Fanny conceal the weapon. Was that Lizzie's other identity–the one that Mary Roberts had quizzed her about? Had Red Bull somehow suspected Lizzie had used another name? Had he threatened to go to the authorities to get her an even longer sentence? Jennie'd keep that question to herself – for now.

"Lizzie said something about Red Bull telling lies," Jennie said. She crinkled her brow in thought. "What if he lied to get this job, and Lizzie threatened to tell on him? So then Red Bull made up the story about her planning a mutiny and told the captain to keep her from talking."

Fanny picked up the thread of the story. "She'd be wild when she found out he was one of her guards. This would be the first time she's come across him since she saw him at the Old Bailey."

"That would make sense," Jennie agreed. "But why would he beat her so cruelly?"

Fanny shrugged. "Because he could. Because he's nasty." She paused. "Or maybe Lizzie tried to blackmail him for money, and he wanted to keep her quiet."

"She'd do that?"

Fanny gave her a scornful look. "What better hold to have over a guard?"

"Well, it didn't work out so well," said Jennie.

"Pfff, that's for sure," said Fanny. She set the bowl of water on the floor beside the guardroom door and gave a light tap, then moved away quickly.

Jennie hurried to return the salve to the surgery. She wondered if Lizzie and Maggie were the same person—and what crime Red Bull had committed.

Jennie barely made it back to her bunk when Meadows bellowed, "Everyone on deck!"

"Just in time for a promenade," said Sarah with a pat on Jennie's shoulder.

Despite a sense of foreboding about Lizzie, when Jennie poked her head out of the hatchway, she felt some relief for the first time in ages. The air was fresh, it wasn't raining and escaping from the fetid stench of days in the ship's bowels gave her a nudge of hope.

CHAPTER TEN

ANOTHER WEEK or two passed, or so Jennie thought – she'd lost count. The weather was intermittently balmy with temperate breezes and cool with brisk winds sweeping down from the north. The sky always seemed to be overcast, and the water churned grey on the horizon. Although there were some reprieves of sun-smudged days with hot zephyrs off the northwestern tip of the African coast, they never lasted long.

Jennie knew they were heading toward Tenerife, but it seemed to be taking a long time. In a way this was tolerable, as she still hadn't come up with an escape plan. She, Alice and Fanny nursed Lizzie, and the infected wounds began healing. Hildy and Gladys bickered next to her on a daily basis, often about Flo.

"Flo's such a lying bilker," said Gladys. "I don't know why you always listen to her."

"As if you're not a liar too!" Hildy retorted.

"Don't lump me with the likes of you." Gladys elbowed Hildy.

Jennie squirmed away from them against the hull.

"I wouldn't trust you as far as I could toss you." Hildy shoved Gladys.

"Who do you think you're pushing around, toady?" Hildy

rammed Gladys dangerously close to the edge of the bunk.

"That's enough you two!" Jennie yelped, as Gladys' fist swung past her head. "Don't bring the guards down on us!"

Jennie ducked and curled into a ball as the two women continued tussling and yelling. All at once, they fell off the bunk.

They continued yelling and punching, as the other women egged them on. Jennie slid to the edge of the bunk and peered over. Flo tried to pull them apart and got kicked in the process. She bent over clutching her shin.

"Stop it now!" Sarah grabbed a flailing arm and yanked hard.

She hauled Hildy off Gladys. Hildy drew back as if to strike Sarah, but Sarah slapped her across the face. Hildy jolted back in surprise.

Jennie was shocked too. She hardly noticed that Flo had recovered and dragged Gladys out of the fray.

"I'll do it again, if you don't stop this nonsense," Sarah threatened. Wheezing hard, she glared at Gladys and then at Hildy. Her frizzy hair stuck out like a huge bird's nest on her head, almost making Jennie laugh, but the harsh expression on Sarah's face was one that Jennie had never seen before. She kept silent.

"Just like children squabbling over nothing," Sarah admonished, her face flushed, her eyes blazing.

Gladys and Hildy glared at each other, rubbing at their sore spots and scratches.

"Say your apologies, before the guards come," Sarah ordered as she glanced down the aisle. "Too late!"

Jennie leaned out for a better look. Three guards stood, conferring at the bottom of the ladder, their conversation drifting toward her.

"Neither of them wins. I keep the wager," said Scarface.

"Not fair!" said Red Bull. "The fat hag didn't let them finish their fight."

Scarface started up the ladder, but Red Bull grabbed his leg.

"You got no right to keep it!"

"I told you neither would win. I keep it!" Scarface jerked himself free and bolted up the ladder. Red Bull and Walt followed on his heels, protesting.

Jennie drew back onto the bunk, astonished. The guards had been betting on the outcome of Gladys and Hildy's fight. Had the bet been a lot of money?

Jennie rolled herself tight to the hull as the three subdued women joined her. She hoped peace would reign for a while now. The three, when they got along, left Jennie out of their conversations, which suited her fine. She stayed clear of them, and from Iris too. Her praying had become louder and included waving her hands in the air in the hopes of getting God's attention.

When Jennie wasn't pounding around the deck or carrying out chores, she joined Sarah and Alice, or sometimes Kate, for short, listless chats. But for the most part, she took to her berth to be alone and let her mind drift to fading thoughts of home.

ONE MORNING Sarah gently shook Jennie's hand that hung over the edge of the bunk. "Ducky, time to go."

Jennie's bunkmates were nowhere to be seen. She hadn't heard the bell or the shipmate's bellow to assemble for their morning stretch. Nor had she noticed the others leaving. Dazed, Jennie blinked and automatically edged down with her mattress, stumbling in line behind Sarah and Alice. Sarah's voice and Alice's chatter seemed to come from some place in the distance.

When she poked her head out of the hatch, the sky was lightening. A silver sheen blanketed the water. As they rounded the stern, she fixed her face toward the sun breaking into streaks of rosy red on the horizon.

"The sky is so pretty," said Alice close beside her.

Jennie remembered a similar daybreak at her childhood cottage when her father had tiptoed into her room. Finding her awake, he carried her to the window seat where they gazed at the dawn together and listened to the first trill of songbirds.

"Aye, that it is, but with it comes a dire warning," Kate said, breaking into Jennie's thoughts. "Red sails at night, sailor's delight. Red sails in the morning, sailor's warning." She peered uneasily over her shoulder and made the sign of the cross.

A sudden whistle of wind rushed over them.

From behind them, Fanny said, "I don't like the feel of that."

"Indeed, it's ominous," Sarah agreed.

Jennie felt the little hairs lift at the back of her neck.

After only a couple of marching rounds, stronger gusts swept across the deck, flapping the sails and buffeting the prisoners. Meadows was on the bridge with his sextant. Coombs clung to his perch on the masthead as the ship bobbed and dipped.

"Tighten the centreboard winch, hoist the mizzenmast and lower the boom," Lieutenant Yates bellowed. Then he ordered Coombs down.

Jennie's chest tightened as the sail whipped around and nearly knocked Coombs off the mast. He clung with one hand until he managed a better hold, and finally made it to the deck.

"Look at the sky now!" Alice pointed to massive dark clouds rolling overhead, blocking out the dawn.

An instant wind sent the sails snapping wildly. Flecks of foam leapt against the ship.

"Look lively!" shouted Lieutenant Yates. "All hands on deck!"

Sailors scrambled to steady the sails, tightening the winches. A flash of lightning split the sky. A roll of thunder and a sudden upsurge of wind sent the sails flapping erratically, and then a torrent of rain bombarded them.

Iris clasped her hands in prayer. Women gathered in tight

groups on the rain-splashed deck. In seconds, everyone was drenched. Even Red Bull was too busy wiping the rain out of his eyes to peer at Jennie's dress plastered to her body. He surprised her even more when he grasped Walt, before the man tumbled with a sudden pitch of the ship, and guided him out of the wind.

Meadows bellowed, "Get the prisoners below deck!"

Nate ran to lift the hatch cover as the warders herded the prisoners below. Again the vessel lurched in the crashing waves. Jennie, for once, was grateful to be heading safely below. Nate saved her from falling when Reverend Brantford thrust past her and pushed aside some of the other women and children. Jeers followed him as he scuttled down first.

Halfway down the wet ladder, Jennie's foot slipped. She tumbled, landing on a heap of other women who had suffered a similar fate. The hatch door slammed down after the last of them. Jennie shivered down the dark passageway, wiping the rain off her face and wringing her hair. Sarah pulled Jennie into the bottom berth where she, Kate and Alice huddled, teeth chattering. Pockets of women gathered in berths that others had temporarily vacated, all wanting to be with the ones they had befriended.

Iris bunked in with Mary Roberts, who complained loudly, "Where's your bloody God now, I ask you? Fat lot of good he's doing any of us!"

"The Lord will preserve us!" Iris croaked, and then she was silent.

The lashing of wind and scraping of timbers went on for hours. In the hold, the livestock bellowed and bawled. There was no sound from the guardroom, nor did the guards venture out to check on them. Jennie and her companions held tightly to the rails of their berths and each other to keep from sliding off.

Kate and several others, struck with sudden bouts of vomiting, lurched down the passageway barely able to stay upright.

Many didn't make it to the privies in time.

Amid the stench of vomit, damp straw mattresses, wet hair and half-dried clothing, Jennie fought nausea. Occasionally she heard shouts above board between the rumbles of thunder and the pummelling rain. The wind continued to whistle sharply around the ship. Across the passageway, Jennie eyed an extinguished lantern swinging violently. She was about to suggest someone grab it, when it broke off its peg and crashed into the corner of a berth, narrowly missing a small child.

Abruptly, the storm stilled. An eerie silence fell over the prisoners. Jennie's heart thudded. Was the tempest over at last?

Moments later, loud booms of thunder returned. Crashing waves ripped at the ship as if it was a fragile toy that might break at any second. Jennie's throat tightened as she tried to swallow. The ship's timbers screeched.

Alice clung tightly to Jennie, and Sarah squeezed them both. Kate grasped Jennie's free hand, praying to the blessed saints to save them all. In the next berth, women sang quietly to themselves. Jennie heard them over Iris screaming her prayers. Jennie prayed too – silently and fervently – expecting any moment that lightning would strike the ship and they'd be consumed by fire as in her early nightmares.

Throughout the night, the ship heaved and thunder roared. Jennie and the others held themselves fast in their bunks. They snatched odd moments of sleep, only to be jolted awake by the intense pitching of the ship.

Jennie figured it must be nearing morning, when suddenly, the ship heaved upright. She reeled against Alice. Sarah cried out as she and Kate ripped through the tattered lee cloths that were supposed to hold them in their bunks and they fell off their berth in a heap. Alice rolled and plunked on top of them. With another plunge of the ship, Jennie landed on the floor beside them.

Moments later, mops, brooms, lanterns and wooden pails

broke loose from their moorings and clattered down the passageway. Jennie yelped when a pail hit her on the head. As she pushed it away and righted herself, she heard a horrible groaning sound. Then something smashed against the hull. Several more cracking sounds from within the hold followed with more loud bangs.

"There go the benches and tables!" shrieked someone near the ladder. Women in the hammocks above screamed as they were flung wildly about. Some crashed to the floor when the fastenings let go.

Frantic shouts came from above. "Batten down the hatches!"

Jennie stiffened. Although she didn't know exactly what that meant, she did know something was horribly wrong. She heard pounding around the hatch and then something being dragged over top of it.

Women and children from the far end of the passageway screamed and cried, as they rushed to the ladder and began pounding on the hatch cover. "They've locked us in!"

The guardroom door flew open. A crack of light shone behind Red Bull's dark bulk clinging to the door frame.

"What the bloody hell!" he hollered.

Behind him Nate braced himself, his face drained and hollow in the shallow light.

Red Bull bellowed a string of profanities, as he plunged down the passageway, pushing the women out of his way. His eyes bulged with fear. He thumped at the hatch cover and bellowed, "Let us out, you bastards!"

"No good," Walt yelled at him from behind the women who had pushed toward the ladder. "If they open the hatch, the water will come in for sure, and the boat will go down!"

"Stand back, all of you," ordered Scarface, shoving his way through the crush. "Back to your berths. Lash yourselves in!"

The guards elbowed their way through the convicts and

congregated at the base of the ladder, clinging to it tighter with each pitch of the ship. Children howled as people crashed against one another, struggling back to their berths.

"Are we going to drown?" cried Alice, throwing herself at Jennie.

Jennie looked across at Sarah and Kate, rigid with terror. "No," she told the trembling child in as firm a voice as she could manage. She helped Alice, as Sarah and Kate crawled back into their berth. All of them barely kept from plunging to the floor.

The shrieking of the wind increased. The ship dipped severely to one side, then tilted toward the other. Jennie was panic-stricken. Was all to be lost? Was she going to die?

CHAPTER ELEVEN

FOR HOURS THE SHIP plunged and reared in the raging storm. Jennie and the others held tight in their berths as best they could as the waves and wind battered the ship. Everyone prayed in earnest, even those who vowed never to pray again, though Iris was loudest. Jennie prayed too, for their survival, and to see her family again.

Abruptly, the roar of thunder ceased, as did the shrilling of the wind. The bellowing of the livestock below and the moaning of the timbers persisted, as the ship continued to rock and roll in the crashing waves, but the hurricane seemed to have passed.

"Is it over?" asked Alice.

"No," Sarah whispered hoarsely, her body stiff against Jennie.

They waited. Fear grabbed Jennie so tightly she couldn't breathe. All at once there was a giant sucking sound.

"Brace yourselves!" Nate yelled from somewhere down the passageway.

Moments later, the ship's prow tilted straight out of the seething ocean and smacked back down, jolting everyone. Immediately the ship rose again on another massive wave. It twisted, lurched sideways and smashed into something with a horrible, wrenching shudder. The ship lifted again, trembled, and dropped suddenly. Then came the splintering of wood followed by a terrible roar.

Suddenly, the sound of the storm magnified, and Jennie caught a glimpse of jagged rocks. As the ship tilted, she saw angry black clouds. A second later, a wave blotted out the sky. There was a gaping hole in the hull where the galley had been!

Before anyone could react, water poured into the hold, whooshing down the passageway. Those in the hammocks just below the rupture never knew what hit them. They lay in the path of the rushing water that swept them along until they were wedged against something solid. Screaming women rushed to the stern and climbed to higher berths.

Jennie scrambled upright and helped Alice to stand. She sloshed through ankle deep water as she pushed her friends into higher bunks nearby, then hung back.

"What are you doing?" Sarah yelled.

"I have to find Lizzie!" Jennie turned toward the cells and was pushed along by the clamouring knot of women.

"Stay with us, Jennie!" Alice shouted after her.

But Jennie took no heed. When she caught sight of Red Bull clinging to a top berth in the guardroom, she screamed at him, "Open the jail cells!"

"Do it yourself," Red Bull snarled. He flung the keys down.

All of a sudden Nate was by her side. He snatched the keys from the floor and raced to open the cell doors.

"Get to a higher place," he yelled at her, but Jennie followed him, as he hurried to shepherd the women out of the cells.

At last she saw Lizzie, struggling to keep upright as the press of women carried her along. Jennie snatched Lizzie's hand. The ship tilted, throwing them against the berths. Pain shot through Jennie's shin and hip. She clenched her teeth and pulled Lizzie with her, wedging her way through a crushing bottleneck of women.

Jennie gave up trying to get back to her friends. Instead, she thrust Lizzie upwards into a berth that was already crammed full. Reaching hands pulled them both up. Eleven women were jammed together with Jennie, shaking in fear and mumbling prayers.

"Do you have a safe place?" Alice yelled, her voice wavering above the sound of rushing water.

Jennie assured her she was safe, though she knew this was far from the truth.

All around them the wind howled and the waves continued to pound against the ship. The sea rushed in faster, aided by a wind-blown blast of icy, pelting rain. Jennie became numb with cold. They watched and waited as the water level rose to the bottom berths, then ever higher. The sounds of livestock below had ceased long before. When would their time come?

"We can't just wait to drown. We have to do something." Jennie heard Nate from farther along the berths where the guards had lodged.

Walt answered, "What would you have us do, lad? There's nowhere to go."

"We've crashed onto rocks, there must be land. At least we'd have a better chance than sitting here."

Walt agreed. "Check if you have the will," he said. "You go on, lad. I'll wait here for you to report back."

"What about the rest of you?" Nate asked.

"Can't swim." The answer came from several of them.

"Not even you, Coombs? Edwards? You're sailors!" Nate chided.

"Doesn't mean we can swim."

Jennie was surprised Coombs and Edwards hadn't been on deck with the rest of the crew. They must have joined the guards to play cards and been trapped.

"We're all going to drown," said Coombs, fear evident in his voice.

"Not if I can help it," Nate replied.

Jennie heard a splash. Moments later, Nate appeared, pulling himself along the edge of the upper berths, his legs submerged in the icy water. Jennie watched in amazement and dread as he made his way toward the yawning rupture.

Somehow he found purchase above the swirling sea. He struggled against the force of the incoming water that dragged at his body. He lost his grip and the surge swept him back.

Again, he grabbed for a hold and half-swam, half-pulled himself through the sluicing water. Clutching the ragged, broken boards at the edge of the opening, he hoisted his upper torso through. Nate kicked hard and strained to hang on as he surveyed the scene for a few minutes. At last he dropped down and let himself be carried back by the current.

Nate took a deep breath and disappeared below the water. He was under so long that Jennie thought he had drowned. But he reappeared, clutching the end of a torn hammock. He made his way to a post and secured the end ropes around it. Then he dove again and pulled up another hammock. He tied it to the first.

Several more times Nate fought his way underwater and back again, making a length of hammocks that he stretched and dragged toward the opening. Somehow he managed to secure the last one to the broken boards. He pulled himself along it, testing it for sturdiness, then stopped, clinging to a post.

"For anyone who would like to try, it'll be safer on deck," Nate shouted. "I don't know how we'll survive once we're out of the hold, but we're sure to die if we stay here."

"What's it like topside, lad?" hollered Walt.

"The ship is rammed onto the rocks, so it shouldn't shift for a time, unless the storm worsens."

"I say we try it!" Sarah yelled. "Jennie, are you up for it?"

"Oh, yes!" she called back.

"I'll help," said Walt. He splashed into the water and edged along the top berths the way Nate had done.

The water was higher now, and his going was slow. Several women dropped into the water and headed toward the opening, hampering one another as they rushed to be saved. Many hung back, too terrified to move. Red Bull overtook the women one by one, almost throwing them out of his way as he thrashed to the opening. When he passed Jennie, he had terror in his eyes.

Nate shouted more instructions. "When you get up top, stay together in the centre in case the ship tilts."

The others from Jennie's berth rushed to save themselves ahead of her and Lizzie. A shocking jolt of frigid water hit Jennie as she lowered herself over the edge of the bunk. She reached back for Lizzie.

"You go. I'll only hinder you," Lizzie said, hanging back.

"I'm not going without you." Jennie yanked Lizzie's hand and pulled her down.

Lizzie sputtered and cursed, as Jennie shoved her against the berth ahead of them. Jennie grabbed a wrist and forced Lizzie to hold on to the edge.

"We'll never make it," Lizzie protested.

"Not if we don't try."

Lizzie inched her way along.

"A little faster," Jennie urged, as the water reached her waist.

They struggled down the length of the berths, fighting against the water. Ahead, Nate and Walt struggled to push the women through the opening where water continued to gush in. As Jennie neared them, she saw hands reaching to pull the women above board. Who had gone ahead of Nate and Walt to help? Red Bull's beefy arms were swarthy, and the ones helping were slender.

Jennie pressed forward. There were so many of them to go

yet. At last Lizzie was shoved up, and it was Jennie's turn. She hung on tight, pulling as hard as she could as the men battled against the surge to thrust her upwards. Strong hands grabbed her wrists and yanked her onto the deck. She lay there stunned, as ominous grey clouds swirled above her.

Jennie wiped the moisture off her face. Whoever had helped her was reaching for the next person. When he turned, she saw it was Meadows. How had he been saved? Then Sarah was there helping her stand. Jennie let herself be guided to the centre of the deck, keeping low to help against the pitching and rolling of the ship.

When Jennie reached the huddle of women, Alice and Kate hugged her and pulled her beside them. Sarah started back to help others.

Kate touched her arm. "I'll take a turn. You need a rest."

Sarah shook her head. "There's not much time left."

"We'll both go then," said Kate.

"I can go too," volunteered Jennie.

"No," said Kate. "We can only get people out one at a time, anyway."

"She's right, you rest," said Sarah. "Though another strong man would be nice to relieve Meadows." She nodded toward Red Bull, who skulked in the shadows of the damaged wheelhouse, his back to the rescue efforts.

Kate and Sarah somehow kept their balance as they staggered back to the gaping hole, only to find that Coombs and Edwards had made it out, and were now helping to rescue the others. They returned to the group of women.

Jennie crushed herself tight to them to keep warm. They were quite a big group by now, but three quarters of the prisoners still needed to get out. Jennie knew the water was rising quickly, and they wouldn't all make it. She stared in shock at her surroundings. The mast closest to the stern had snapped off and the largest sail dangled precariously by ropes over the starboard. The poop deck and quarterdeck were gone, as was the top of the captain's cabin. And so was the rest of the crew.

"How did Meadows survive?" she asked.

"Apparently he was in the captain's quarters and somehow got trapped there when the ship hit the rocks. Fortunate for him, but not for Captain Furlee and Lieutenant Yates, who were swept away in the wreckage," said Fanny.

"Fortunate for us. He's here to guide us," said Jennie. "Nate and the others too."

Alice said, "The reverend and the surgeon were meeting with the captain as well, and they're gone."

Jennie stretched to see beyond the huge, jagged rocks impaling the ship on its port side. Cautiously she stood, propping her hands on Alice's shoulders to keep from falling over. Some distance past a large number of rocks, she could see a ledge that might offer some shelter, though the danger to get there would be great. Only the agile were likely to make it.

She settled back down, and Alice tapped her shoulder. "What did you see?"

Jennie explained the situation to a silent group of women. They stared at the roiling sea as the wind whistled around them. Though they might have been saved from drowning below deck, they were still facing great peril. They needed to find food and water. The chance of being rescued was unlikely, as they had been blown far off course.

A feeling of absolute hopelessness overcame Jennie.

CHAPTER TWELVE

The wind and the waves, relentless under the darkening sky, continued to pound the crippled ship.

Suddenly, the vessel shifted with a groan. Everyone screamed and scrabbled for a hold. The mass of women plummeted to starboard grabbing onto whatever they could: cleats, ropes, fallen sails, broken masts. Several tumbled overboard.

Jennie lost her grip on Alice, but she was lucky enough to roll against the hatch door and was able to hold on to its latch. Through the melee, Jennie glimpsed Sarah and Alice clutching the capstan not far away. Sarah had a gash on her forehead, but she and Kate struggled to tie the three of them to the capstan with the end of a frayed rope. It might hold them in place, but if the ship capsized, nothing would save them.

Behind her, someone whimpered. Jennie turned to find Lizzie clinging to a useless mooring rope. Although the ship still rocked ominously, for now the ship seemed to have stabilized somewhat from the major shift. Jennie reached for Lizzie and dragged her over. They tied themselves to the latch.

Jennie looked toward the yawning rent where Meadows was lying flat on his stomach with Coombs and Edwards beside him. They had roped themselves to the splintered boards protruding from the breach, and were reaching for someone. Was it Nate? Or Walt? Maybe they would have a chance to get out even though the water had probably reached the top of the second deck.

The men heaved and Walt's bedraggled body slumped onto the deck. Rolling Walt over and out of the way, they reached down again. Nate emerged, coughing and spluttering. Meadows said something to him and Nate shook his head. The men collapsed on the deck, breathing hard.

Jennie knew the rest of the women were gone. She whispered a silent prayer for all those who hadn't been saved. Then she surveyed what was left of the group that had made it out and hadn't toppled overboard. Only about thirty of them remained. Jennie wondered what they would do next. They wouldn't survive long without food or water. And she knew none of them could withstand another lashing from waves if the weather worsened.

As the ship settled, Jennie realized that for some reason the aft end seemed to be floating with just the main deck above the water line. She wondered how long that would last and how long they would keep getting battered by repercussions of the hurricane. The churning waves seemed to go on endlessly. It might take days before the sea calmed after such a furious storm.

Jennie turned to see Meadows and Nate making their way on their hands and knees, dragging a rope and periodically tying it to the cleats along the bulwark – another provision for people to hang on to or guide them, if the weather turned ferocious again. When the men got to the jolly boat, they rose to inspect it, then moved to the long boat. Both crafts were intact. Jennie felt a surge of hope. Maybe they could get off the ship with those, but there were too many of them to all fit. They would have to make two trips if they were going to try to reach the rocks.

Jennie slumped back. What good would getting to the rocks

and ledge do? There was nowhere to go from there, and they would soon perish with no food or water. She ran a tongue over her parched lips. She just wanted to lie down in a soft, warm bed and sleep.

Suddenly, Red Bull rose from the shadows of the shattered wheelhouse. He lumbered toward Meadows and Nate. Their shouts could be heard above the wind.

"No, we stick together!" Meadows yelled. "We'll work out how to get everyone on the boats, but not until we're properly prepared."

"But it would be faster for me to go without any extra weight. I could bring back help," insisted Red Bull.

Jennie felt a surge of anger. Trust him to try and save himself first. They'd never see him again if he left. He cared only for himself.

Meadows knew it too. "No! We need to find food and water to take with us. Anyway, you wouldn't be able to row alone."

"I'd manage. Besides, we already know there's nothing here," said Red Bull.

"We'll have to find what we can below deck," said Nate. "You can help with that."

Red Bull snorted and whirled away. "I'll check what's left of the captain's quarters."

"There'll be naught of significance there," said Meadows. "The hurricane will have carried everything away."

Red Bull took no heed, and scurried as fast as he could to the captain's quarters before they could stop him.

"I'll dive below deck to see if I can find water and food, sir," Nate offered. "I'll need a line around my waist and someone to pull me and whatever I can find up when I tug."

"I'll do it," said Meadows, glancing over at Walt's prone body. "Walt doesn't look like he's up for much. Coombs and Edwards can help too."

"I can help," said Jennie, untying herself. "I can swim...and hold my breath for a long time too."

"You're just a girl," said Meadows.

"Let me at least see what I can salvage from the surgery. We may need it and I'll know what to bring," Jennie petitioned.

Reluctantly Meadows agreed. "We don't have much time in any case," he said. "There's no telling how long the ship will stay afloat."

Jennie had a sudden thought about what it would be like in the hold. There would be floating bodies and the thought of what she might touch made her feel queasy. Presumably the water pulsing in had carried the bodies toward the aft, but there was no telling what the currents had done. She'd try to stay in contact with the hull as much as she could.

She and Nate secured ropes around their middles. Nate went down first. He caught Jennie by the waist as she lowered herself into the hold. Closing her eyes, she took a deep breath and dove beneath the frigid water. She grabbed blindly for anything solid. Once or twice she felt something bulky and soft bump against her and she kicked it away, knowing that it might be a body, but she didn't dare open her eyes to see. Finally she felt what she thought was the bulkhead and kept in touch with it until she'd reached what she hoped was the doorway of the surgery. She felt along the wall where the shelves of medicines should be. There was nothing! They had to have fallen to the floor, but she was almost out of air. She whirled and swam back to the opening, gasping for breath as she broke the surface.

"Anything?" Meadows asked. Coombs and Edwards stood by with grim faces.

"Not yet." She took several deep breaths and plunged again. This time she reached the surgery quicker and felt along the floor until her hands touched a tin. It had to be the lard for salve. She tucked it under her arm, but found it difficult to swim back with it.

She thrust it at Meadows when she came up for another breath. "I need something to carry things in," she panted.

Nate emerged beside her, puffing. "I think I've found a keg of drinking water, but we'll need ropes or a harness of some kind. And lots of strength topside for hauling it up."

"We'll cut some pieces of rope," said Meadows, withdrawing a pocketknife. "Coombs, get Chilcott to help us haul the barrel. Walt and Edwards, come with me."

"Who's Chilcott?" Jennie asked Nate through chattering teeth.

"Your Red Bull," he said. "That vile man, who somehow lives while others didn't make it." Nate's words echoed Jennie's thoughts.

A couple of minutes passed while Nate and Jennie stayed in the water, shivering. At last the men returned with several lengths of rope, fashioned into a rough harness for the keg with long ropes at either end for hauling.

"This is the best we could do," Meadows said. "Chilcott refused to come, but Walt will do what he can to help. So will the women." Meadows handed the makeshift carrier to Nate.

Eyes closed, Nate guided Jennie to the located barrel. Nate tipped the heavy keg while Jennie slipped the knot of ropes underneath. He took half the ropes, while she took the other three. As fast as they could, they swam to the top with all the rope ends, handing them to the waiting men above deck.

"Pull hard," Nate ordered.

At first they only managed to budge the barrel. They all strained harder. At last it moved more easily and finally appeared at the opening. It took all of the men to lift it out of the water and onto the deck.

"I didn't find much in the way of food, but I'll check again,"

Nate reported.

Jennie grappled in the water beside him. "I need to find more medicines, but I can't carry them. Can we stick them in your pockets?"

Nate nodded. "Come on, just this one last time. We'll look for both."

Although Jennie and Nate searched, they only found a few containers of medicines and a leather pouch. There was no food that hadn't been spoiled beyond use.

When they were topside again, the women clustered around Jennie, rubbing her arms and shoulders to warm her up. Jennie retrieved the leather pouch and medicines from Nate. She assessed the finds, tucked them into the pouch then joined Sarah to tend the gash on her forehead.

The men opened the keg of water and gave everyone a rationed drink. Jennie had never tasted anything so good. She savoured the trickle, moistening her lips and rolling it around her mouth before swallowing.

Finally, she joined Lizzie, who had opened the hatch cover and tied herself more securely to it. She helped as Jennie did the same. Jennie tied the medicine pouch around her waist, and they settled in to wait for whatever measures they would take next.

The fresh water revived them all for a short time. There wasn't nearly enough to quench their thirsts, and Jennie's stomach ached from hunger. Worse, she was continually wet, and the cold had seeped into her bones. She wondered if she would ever be warm again.

In a fog, Jennie watched Nate and the other men secure the barrel of drinking water to a solid part of the ship and pile items by the jolly and long boats. Nate disappeared below deck again, fishing out anything he could find that might be useful, while Coombs and Edwards collected and sorted them.

The weather turned on them again in a fury. Jennie hunched against the onslaught of wind and rain as dark, swirling clouds loomed overhead. The gale increased, driving the salty spray in blinding sheets across the ship. Jennie's heart pounded as she gulped ragged breaths. There was nowhere to take shelter, and all she could do was hang on.

She and Lizzie braced themselves as a towering wave crashed over the entire ship. Horrified, Jennie saw women and children, who were not securely tethered, being swept off the deck and into the churning ocean. As the wave receded, Jennie and Lizzie spluttered beside each other. Before they had time to recover, another massive wave knocked the ship sideways. The hatch lid tore from its hinges and ripped out of Jennie's hands. She felt herself flying through the air with Lizzie still clinging to her. As the ship's bow smashed down, Lizzie's grip loosened.

When Jennie slammed onto the watery deck, a searing pain shot up her right side. She landed near Alice, Sarah and Kate, still bound to the capstan, bedraggled and sobbing. Lizzie had been flung against a railing; she grabbed onto the ropes the men had secured earlier. She fought to make it back to Jennie. Lizzie was almost there, when another fierce wave thundered over them. When it receded, the wave sucked at the stern, lifting the prow straight up out of the ocean. A terrible roar sounded around Jennie as the ship trembled. There was the sound of splintering wood. The vessel gave a violent shudder and the prow broke away from the stern, ripping apart at the gaping hole.

Jennie rolled toward her friends at the capstan, clutching the leather pouch, though it was tied around her waist. The broken halves of the ship heaved into the air. The stern and the bow each inclined steeply in opposite directions, one sliding into the seething sea with a mighty whoosh. The other crashed onto the rocks and broke apart.

Jennie was sluiced into the roiling ocean. The last thing she saw before being submerged was Kate and Sarah struggling to untie the ropes that bound them to Alice and the cracked capstan.

Jennie was flailing in salt water. Her lungs burned; she had no idea which way was up. Surely this was the end.

All at once, a wave heaved her into the air. She snatched a quick breath, and then the frothing sea swallowed her again.

Below the surface of the bubbling water, she briefly saw a plank churn past her. She clawed her way toward it, but the waves pushed and pulled at her. Dizziness overwhelmed her. It was hopeless. A strange calm overcame her as Jenny gave up.

Suddenly something clamped onto her wrist and pulled her upwards. Jennie broke the surface and gasped, her lungs on fire. She paddled wildly, not sure which way to turn. Then a plank was pushed in front of her. Lizzie wrapped Jennie's arms around the board and grabbed hold of the other end.

"Hang on tight!" Lizzie shouted, before another waved rolled over them.

Jennie dug her fingernails into the wood and sucked in a deep breath. When at last she resurfaced, she still clung to the board.

"Lizzie!" she yelled, looking frantically across the scattered debris and floating bodies that stretched as far as she could see.

"Lizzie!" she screamed again. But Lizzie was gone.

Jennie lost her hold on the board, and another wave took her under. When she came up again, she saw a piece of decking that was big enough to crawl up on. Instinctively Jennie kicked her way over. Several times she attempted to climb onto the decking, but slipped off its surface. Thoroughly exhausted, Jennie struggled hard one last time. Scrambling for purchase, she dragged herself up, and collapsed flat on her stomach. As her sodden raft dipped, she realized she had to centre herself on it.

Cautiously, she inched her way to the middle, and the wreckage immediately levelled out, riding the waves more evenly. Only then did Jenny realize the leather pouch was still tied around her waist. Gripping it in her hands, she curled upon her side as great sobs racked her body. The last thing she saw was Lizzie reaching out to her before, utterly miserable and alone, Jennie drifted into darkness.

FOR A MOMENT, Jennie thought she'd gone deaf. The swirling of the sea, though choppy, had calmed considerably. The rain had diminished into huge drops pattering the surface of the agitated sea. The wind had ceased to howl. In its place a ghostly mist rose around her.

From some far-off place, she heard women crying and calling out names of the missing. Jennie rolled onto her belly, her fingers clenched around the end of the makeshift raft. Through the gloom she scanned the frothy sea littered with fragments of the demolished ship, animal carcasses and human bodies. She joined the voices calling for shipmates.

"Sarah, Alice, Kate!" she shouted over and over again. There was no answering call, only cries for help and distant weeping. Jennie kept a strong hold on to the edge of the boards, her head averted from the rain that continued to drench her.

When a stronger wave hit, the raft dipped precariously and Jennie slid into the water. She grabbed for the chunk of decking and held on, pushing and kicking to get as far away from death as possible. Her body was stiff, her progress was slow, but she knew she had to be with the living. Her brain willed her to climb back onto the raft, but she didn't have the strength.

She rested for a few moments, but Lizzie's voice screamed in her head. Jennie gave an involuntary start. Whether it was a dream or reality, Jennie couldn't tell; the suddenness of it shocked her into action. She clawed at the boards with numb fingers, leaned on her elbows and heaved. Her frozen body wouldn't obey her. She tried squirming onto the boards, inching up her chest, her belly, then dug her elbows in and pulled as hard as she could, using the top part of her body for leverage. Squirming and twisting, she at last made some progress. Another effort, and she made it farther. Inch by inch, she wriggled onto the boards. With one more push, she dragged herself entirely up.

Jennie felt nothing, no pain, no fear, no hope, no future. Small laps of water washed over her. Cold seeped into her body. Distant voices faded as, once more, she drifted into oblivion while the dreary mist settled around her in the fading light.

CHAPTER THIRTEEN

"Jennie!"

Thud! Splash!

"Jen-nie!"

Something hard struck Jennie's arm with another splash. Groggily she opened her eyes to bright sunlight. She clasped a hand over her face, squinting from the glare. Water rushed around her as she tilted. She immediately recalled she was on a chunk of wood in the middle of the ocean. *Shipwrecked.*

Lifting her head carefully, she saw Alice and Sarah a few yards away, sitting on a portion of the bow. Alice had a short piece of wood in her hands, which was aimed Jennie's way.

"We roused you, at last!"

Blinking in disbelief, Jennie croaked, "You're alive! Thank God!" Her mouth was so dry, she couldn't swallow.

Cautiously, Jennie sat up. The sun was warm, but she was chilled right through and couldn't stop shivering. At least she wasn't alone any more.

"We're so happy we found you!" Sarah shouted.

"Are you both all right?" Jennie took in the dark gash that had opened up again down Sarah's cheek.

"A few bumps and bruises, but fine," Sarah shouted again.

"We were afraid you were a goner. Good thing this young miss was persistent. She's been whacking her stick and calling you for ever so long."

"I prayed we'd find you safe and here you are," called Alice, beaming.

"Safe as any of us are," said Jennie wryly. She looked for some kind of debris to use as a paddle so she could draw nearer to them.

As if reading her thoughts, Sarah yelled, "Stay put for a bit, pet. We can't have you falling in. We'll wait for Nate to give us a hand." She pointed to a tight group of makeshift rafts dotting the waves.

"Nate?" Jennie craned to see several odd-shaped chunks of ship joined together with bedraggled women balancing on them. Among them she made out a lone male figure in the jolly boat, lashing two chunks together with a rope. Happiness surged through Jennie.

"He's tying us together to prevent us from tipping so easily," Alice called out. "He found pieces of rope and sails among the bigger parts of the ship that got wedged in the rocks. We're gathering whatever we find as we go too, but almost everything sank."

Sarah added, "Nate is still rescuing people and then he'll see about how to transport us all to the rocks."

"Not many can fit on the jolly boat," Jennie noted.

"No. He'll have to take a few at a time. Right now, he needs to be sure he has found all the living," said Sarah.

Jennie studied the small pile of rope on Sarah and Alice's raft.

"Sarah, could you tie a few pieces of rope together and throw them to me?" yelled Jennie. "Maybe we can pull ourselves closer."

Without a word, the pair quickly knotted a few segments together. Sarah coiled the rope in her hand.

"I can do this," Alice said, taking it from the older woman. "I know you won't admit it but your arm is badly banged up. Let me try."

She threw with all her strength, tipping off balance. The rope fell a few feet short and trailed into the water.

"Try again," Jennie encouraged.

This time Alice wound up, gathering momentum, then hurled the rope as hard as she could.

It was closer than the first pitch. Jennie automatically reached out to catch it but leaned too far. She landed in the water with a resounding splash and swallowed a mouthful of salty water. She finally righted herself and twisted the rope around an elbow. Jennie swam back to her board and managed to clamber up. She raised the end of the rope in triumph as Alice and Sarah cheered.

They braced themselves on their knees and on the count of three, began pulling gently but steadily so as not to slide into the sea again. Their floating platforms nudged forward.

Jennie grinned as they came closer and closer together.

"Easy does it, now," said Sarah, as their makeshift rafts butted together and wobbled dangerously.

"We did it!" Alice clapped. She found a splinter on their side and wedged the rope into the crack in the wood. It wasn't terribly secure but it would hold long enough if they were careful not to put too much strain on it.

Jennie had trouble finding anywhere to tie her end of rope. One board jutted out and was quite narrow. She leaned over the edge as far as she dared and wound the rope around it as tightly as she could. She suspected it would slip off before long, but for now she was happy to be close to her friends.

Her thoughts turned to the horrors of the shipwreck. Jennie looked anxiously for other shipmates she'd been close to, but from this distance she couldn't identify anyone.

"Have you seen Kate?" she asked.

Sarah shook her head and turned away.

"She saved our lives," said Alice, "but a big wave took her under, and we couldn't find her. Sarah tried really hard, even with her sore arm."

Sarah pulled Alice tighter to her. "And Lizzie?" she asked.

Tears welled in Jennie's eyes, and she couldn't speak.

"You tried hard to save her too," Alice filled in solemnly.

"She ended up saving me," Jennie croaked out at last. "I tried to –"

Sarah nodded her understanding, and there was a long pause before Jenny could speak again.

"Is Nate the only surviving guard?"

"He's the only one we've seen so far," said Alice. "We did see Meadows and Coombs, but that's it so far for the crew. They're searching for people over there." She pointed behind them. "Oh, look! Nate's headed for us."

Nate handled the jolly boat confidently. Jennie had thought he was meant for the land, yet here he was skilfully manoeuvring in the water.

"We figure Walt and Red Bull went down with the ship," Sarah said. "Otherwise, they'd be helping."

"Probably Red Bull wouldn't help," said Jennie. She couldn't help feeling some relief that Red Bull was gone.

"Nate was really brave," Alice said. "He helped us onto these boards."

Jennie watched Nate coming toward them, poking at floating debris along the way. He reached into the water and pulled out another long stick, then continued on.

"He's looking for firewood," Alice offered. "He says we can dry it out and it will burn so we can send out signals to another ship that might be in the area."

"But drying it could take days." Jennie's teeth chattered;

she trembled with the cold – and with fear. What if they were never rescued?

Puzzled, Jennie asked, "If Nate helped you onto this piece of the ship, and you know what he's planning, why are you here and not tied with the others?"

"He spent most of the night pulling people out of the sea. He didn't start the platform until this morning where several rafts were already close together," said Sarah. "We told him we could wait. He just took one near us. It looks like we're next."

Jennie shifted to watch Nate's approach, and her boards dipped just enough to allow the lapping water to rush over and soak her backside once again. Startled, she realized they could yet sink into the dark depths before someone came to their rescue. If anyone came.

"What about the longboat?" she suddenly remembered.

"Smashed," Alice told her.

"When we're together with the others, we'll come up with a plan," Sarah called with false brightness.

Jennie twigged that Nate had already discovered there was no place to land on the island of rocks and that Sarah was only keeping up Alice's hope.

"Here's Nate now," shouted Alice. She stood up to watch him arrive.

"Easy, ducky," Sarah called to Nate. Fear darted across her features as their inadequate raft jiggled with the movement caused by his arrival. "You know how much I hate being in the water."

As Nate drew closer they heard clanks and rattles that came from a wooden bucket. Dishes, utensils, tools and other bits and bobs poked out of the bucket, along with a battered spyglass from the captain's cabin. Nate had also gathered a pile of rope and sails, and there was a wooden barrel of some kind.

"How on earth did he get all that stuff?" asked Jennie in amazement.

"He gathered it all night as he searched for the survivors," said Sarah. "More of the ship was floating then. Now most everything that might be useful has sunk."

The jolly boat bumped gently up to them.

"Ahoy." Nate smiled when he saw Jennie.

"Hello," Jennie answered.

"I see you've been busy." He studied their tethering. "Instead of towing you," he said, "I'll help you into the boat. There are plenty of other platforms already gathered for you to settle on."

With great care, Nate supported the edge of Jenny's raft as best he could, and she stepped gingerly into the jolly boat, using Nate's shoulders to keep her balance.

"I'm glad you're all right and back." His voice was low.

"You too," she answered as he helped her get seated.

Before she could say anything more, he drew closer to Sarah and Alice. He helped them into the boat, then untied the rope that had held them together and stowed it.

"We'll get you to the main group before you know it," he said.

Jennie was relieved they'd be with the others, and what Nate said about them being together *would* make them safer to some degree. On the other hand, they had no food, no drinking water and no protection from the elements – never mind that there was no sight of land in any direction, except for the small group of craggy rocks that were useless to them.

As if in answer to her unspoken thoughts, Nate said, "Meadows and Coombs are gathering women together in other spots." Looking at Jennie, he added, "Chilcott is searching for provisions."

"It's good news that a few more have survived," said Sarah, though her face was grim. "We've lost so many strong women."

Jennie's eyes widened. Fear crept up her spine. Of all the people who could have died, why was Red Bull not one of them? How could that have happened? Instead sweet, good Kate had perished. There was no justice.

She blamed him too, for Lizzie's dying – not because of the shipwreck. Except for his cruel treatment of her, Lizzie would have been strong enough to have lived. Red Bull was a vile man, and now he was here to plague her. How was she ever going to be able to endure him? She felt even colder than before.

CHAPTER FOURTEEN

JENNIE SHOOK HERSELF back to the present as Nate stopped to poke at something floating nearby. He discarded it, and dipped with strong strokes, headed straight on target for the network of linked, floating boards.

Jennie watched him row. His mouth firmly set, his muscles rippled with each confident tug at the water. Jennie wondered what they would feel like if she touched them. She glanced away before he could catch her staring at him.

She looked toward the horizon. As far as Jennie could see in every direction, wreckage drifted on the dull grey water. She shuddered and kept her eyes averted from the already bloated livestock and floating corpses.

The sun rose higher and warmed her a little. And she felt safer now that she and her friends were in the jolly boat.

Nate called out toward a chunk of ship floating a half a furlong away. "Need any help?" he shouted.

Jennie was relieved to see Coombs with a couple of the Marys.

"Still more over there." Coombs pointed over his right shoulder where two women frantically waved in the distance.

"Can you go for them?" Nate yelled to Coombs.

The sandy-haired man waved acknowledgement and turned

back to the women in his ragtag group.

It took a few minutes to reach the larger group, but when they did, Nate helped Alice and Sarah alight. They made their way to spots where they could balance with the others.

Jennie hesitated. "Could I help you search?"

Nate tilted his head to one side in thought. "Perhaps it would be good to have an extra pair of eyes." He nodded and they set off toward the rocks.

"We'll do another sweep around what's left of the ship," said Nate.

"What's that?" asked Jennie. She'd spied a corner chunk of what was once part of the ship. As they rowed closer she realized it was part of the captain's cabin. "There might be something useful there."

As they drew nearer, they heard thumping.

"Someone must be trapped," said Jennie.

Nate slowed his strokes as they rounded to the open side of the broken structure.

Jennie drew in a sharp breath. A man was trapped between the wall and the heavy overturned captain's desk. With his face turned away, she couldn't tell who it was. His one free hand continued slapping against the wall. He was pinned at the waist, his legs dangling below the water line.

"Ahoy!" Nate called.

The man turned his head slowly toward them. Jennie's gall rose when she saw it was Red Bull.

"Help me," he blubbered.

"What are you doing here?" Nate demanded, as he sized up the situation.

"Looking for supplies," Red Bull whimpered.

"As if there'd be anything in here," said Jennie.

"Up to no good, I've no doubt," agreed Nate. He surveyed the situation some more. "I don't think there's anything we can do.

We'll never be able to move that desk ourselves."

"He doesn't deserve to live anyway." Jennie was surprised by her own wrath.

"That's true." Nate glared at the trapped man.

Red Bull's eyes widened, his face a mask of horror. He started snivelling and begging.

Nate rubbed his fingers on his forehead as if it would help him to think. "I don't think we can just leave him here," he said.

"Why not? He won't last long," said Jennie. She couldn't keep the contempt out of her voice. She had never hated someone so much.

"I don't know how we can get him out."

"I can push with my good arm," Red Bull pleaded. "Please, help me."

Jennie shrunk back behind Nate. Even if they wanted to, there was nothing strong enough to use as leverage.

"I have to try," Nate said, with sudden conviction.

He tied the jolly boat to the leg of a table. With his bare hands he ripped and clawed at a small section of shelving that hung awkwardly above Red Bull's head. He used an oar to pry behind it. He worked at it for quite some time, then was able to yank it off the wall. It fell and landed on the desk, just missing Red Bull's head.

Nate handed the oar back to Jennie and stepped back into the craft. "See if you can keep the boat steady while I push," he said.

Woodenly she obeyed, though her whole being balked. She grabbed the edge of the desk and clung to it to keep the boat as close as she could.

Nate wedged the shelving under the desk and against the wall beside Red Bull. "Now push," he yelled at Red Bull. His weight bore down on the shelving and the desk moved a hair. Red Bull sagged after his first effort.

"Again," Nate hollered. "Harder!"

"Ahhh!" Red Bull strained as Nate used all his force to push on the shelf.

The desk suddenly shifted, and Red Bull slipped down into the ocean. Nate held out a piece of board for Red Bull to latch onto. He came up spluttering and almost pulled Nate into the water. Nate struggled to right himself and snatched Red Bull by the collar. Finally, Nate managed to get Red Bull into the boat. Jennie scurried to move buckets and rope to make room for him.

Red Bull grunted and groaned and rubbed his legs.

"Your legs will be fine; they're just numb," Nate told him curtly. "You don't know how lucky you are to come out of that with only a few cuts and scrapes."

Jennie made sure she didn't look at Red Bull as Nate rowed toward the group of women waiting for them. How was she ever going to endure the horrible man? He would always be there to plague her.

Jennie and Nate made their way to the stranded women as quickly as they could. Every time Red Bull opened his mouth to complain, Nate told him to shut it. Jennie was grateful she didn't have to listen to him, and she vowed to stay as far away from him as possible.

At last they reached the lashed-together group of makeshift rafts. Once they secured themselves to the others and transferred Red Bull, Jennie scanned the nine or so women quickly. She waved at Fanny toward the back. Fanny gave her a little salute and a grin. Iris was on her knees in the middle of a raft, praying and caterwauling. Jennie didn't know any of the others well. But none of her bunkmates were there. No babies or children at all. Grief for the terrible loss enveloped her.

Looking around, Jennie saw the superb job Nate had done stringing the odd floating pieces together. He had sorted little stockpiles of supplies they might need. Bits of sails and other items were laid out to dry. Thank goodness Nate had taken charge the way he had.

Everything with the injured seemed to be under control too. One woman tended another who was lying flat on her back. Some had strips of sail bandaging heads and legs or arms. Jennie felt for her medicine pouch. It was still secure if she needed it. Maybe she should look at Sarah's gash.

"I'm fine, pet," said Sarah, when Jennie offered. She pressed the back of a plump hand to her forehead.

"At least let me clean it."

Sarah gave in. "Thank you," she said, patting Jennie's arm when she'd finished.

"You should be healed in no time." Alice beamed.

Jennie made the rounds of the other injured women and administered salve where needed. A needle and sutures would have come in handy too, but she had none. As she neared Red Bull, she turned away. Someone else could tend to him. He would have no sympathy from her.

She joined Sarah and Alice, sitting in the middle of their raft. With all the bobbing rafts tied tightly, they were somewhat stabilized, as long as care was taken to evenly distribute their weight.

Suddenly Alice shouted, "What's that?"

Jennie stared at white flecks on the horizon, shielding her eyes with her hands.

Nate grabbed the battered spyglass. He stared for several moments. Jennie watched, as the white specks grew slightly bigger. Nate whistled loudly to the other men who were still searching out on the open water.

"Ship Ahoy! Ship Ahoy!" he yelled, ripping off his shirt and waving wildly.

Jennie joined everyone shrieking and waving their arms at the sailing ship coming in their direction.

"We're saved," Jennie shouted, as tears streamed down her face.

"That ship sure is taking its time getting here," said Alice, after what seemed a very long wait.

"Aye, there's no wind. It appears totally becalmed," said Sarah.

With the rescue ship almost dead in the water until there was wind, their relief would be delayed.

In the meantime the two crewmen arrived with Hildy and one of the Marys. Nate helped the exhausted women onto the floating platform. When Meadows made the jolly boat secure and stepped onto the raft, Jennie was actually glad to see him. As a ranking member of the crew, he'd been brusque with his orders but always fair and not unkind to her. Farther afield, Nate had gathered one other survivor and headed back toward them. Edwards was with him and had helped him row.

Overhead high, grey clouds began to drift into sight on the wings of a breeze. Jennie warily looked at the sky. A chill swept over her. *Please don't let it rain. Please let the ship get here first. Please let the wind pick up – but not too much. Please don't let us capsize.*

When the rescue ship at last came into full view, Jennie could see it was narrower than the *Emily Anne* and had massive square rigging with a black hull and a white stripe.

"It's a Blackwell Frigate – a clipper ship," Meadows identified the three-masted vessel.

Jennie didn't care what kind of ship it was; only that it hadn't been a mirage, and they would soon be on it.

Alice stood up and watched it approach. "It's coming faster now."

The wind had increased, but by no means did it warrant the ship's need for such a fast approach. Jennie watched as it bore down on them.

"Isn't that too fast?" asked Alice.

"Right you are, luv," said Sarah in alarm.

Jennie clasped her hands over her chest, watching with disbelief as the ship maintained its speed.

"Gawd almighty!" Meadows gawked at the ship's approach. "It's not stopping! Everyone hang on to something."

"Get down, hang on!" Nate yelled. "The wake is going to hit us!"

Everyone dropped flat onto the rafts, shrieking and grabbing the edges and each other. Sarah pulled Jennie down and protected Alice.

Jennie was amazed when the frigate suddenly tacked to the side and made a wide berth around them. The name on its side was obscured, and there was nothing else to identify it. Women began screaming and waving when they realized they might not be saved after all. Jennie heard herself moan.

"Bloody hell!" Meadows cursed some more and stared after the ship in astonishment.

"Here come the waves!" he yelled. "Stay down."

The water undulated wildly toward them. Jennie grabbed a tied rope with one hand and drew in her friends with the other. Wave after wave crashed over them, spinning them out of control.

When the sea finally calmed, Jennie raised her head. Sarah and Alice were still with her. She rose slowly to survey the damage. Everyone was drenched and shaken, but the joined rafts were still intact. Many of the things they'd collected had been washed away. Curses and sobs filled the air.

"Did we lose anyone?" Meadows shouted.

Several names were reeled off. The din continued as everyone checked to see who was missing.

"Is anyone unaccounted for?" Nate echoed.

Jennie searched for Fanny and Hildy, breathing a sigh of relief when she spotted them. Too bad she also saw Red Bull.

"Why didn't the ship stop for us?" asked Alice through sobs.

A grim look was etched on Nate's face. "Might have been an opium smuggler."

"What difference does that make?" asked Alice, hiccupping back her tears.

"There's a war on. China is trying to stop the British from trading opium illegally," Nate said. "They wouldn't want to be caught nor burdened with the likes of us."

"They could have at least dropped us off somewhere," Alice persisted.

Nate shook his head. "We wouldn't want to be caught up in their battles anyway."

"How could you tell what kind of ship it was?" asked Jennie.

Meadows interjected, "Did you see the flag?"

"It was black with a white skull and crossbones," said Alice.

Sarah asked, "Aren't they sometimes used when a ship has been quarantined because of disease or death?"

"Or else a smuggler or pirate ship," Meadows added. "Usually something not lawful or healthy."

A shiver raced across Jennie's shoulders. She looked at Nate. His nod was slight.

"That's a really bad thing isn't it?" Alice's eyes snapped open wider.

"Yes, it's all bad, my pet," said Sarah, holding her close. She looked over Alice's head at Jennie with fear in her eyes.

Questions poured from the women around them who had heard the discussion. Are we in even more danger? Will someone be following them? Will there be cannons? Will they kill us?

Jennie started to tremble.

"If someone was chasing them, they'd more than likely be here by now," said Meadows.

Jennie wasn't sure whether to believe him or not. How could he know for sure?

"He's right," Nate assured them.

Still, Jennie wasn't convinced. She gazed at the northern

horizon. The sky was clear. For now.

"Maybe it was better it didn't stop then," said Alice, using her hand to wipe the tears off her face.

Nate didn't say a word.

"Now what's going to happen to us?" whispered Jennie.

"We're going to make it," Nate told her, staring into her eyes, as if willing her to believe him. She sensed that if she did, it would help him believe too. She wanted to trust his words, but she couldn't see how they could be saved. She broke eye contact. All around them, disappointed people moaned and whimpered.

"Let's see what else we might be able to salvage from the ship," Nate said.

Meadows agreed. "We might also check the island of rocks more closely."

Jennie sank down and clasped her arms around her knees. What were the chances that another ship would come their way, and stop for them? She shifted to a more comfortable position. The platform rocked with the rise and fall of rougher waves and a stiffer breeze. The slate clouds hung lower, threatening rain. She rested her chin on her knees and closed her eyes.

CHAPTER FIFTEEN

THE MEN CONTINUED searching, stopping to poke at objects, but there wasn't much of significance except for floating bits of wood. Jennie figured if they had found water or food, they would have announced such a find.

Another horrible thought came to her. What if they found food, but there wasn't enough to go around? How would they decide who got some and who didn't? Who would decide? She took deep breaths and willed her panic down.

That was when Jennie noticed that Red Bull had miraculously recovered and had paddled away on a small raft that had either come untied from the agitation of the waves, or *been* untied during the distraction of the ship's passing. He was quite far from the others, poking around the same portion of the captain's cabin he'd been rescued from, though it had now drifted and the opening had turned toward them.

Jennie averted her head, but kept watching out of the corner of her eye. Red Bull spent a long time searching, glancing furtively around at the whereabouts of the men on the jolly boat and the women on the raft. When he figured they were not looking his way, he slid something into his pocket. He was quick to take up his makeshift paddle again to hide his movements.

Jennie thought about confronting Red Bull when he returned, but remembered too well his cruel streak and the despicable things he'd done to Lizzie. He'd lie and deny it. How she loathed the man! She had to avoid him at all costs. Her curiosity was roused though. What had he hidden away? Maybe she'd mention it to Nate, instead.

"Oh my God, look!" Hildy shrieked and pointed behind them.

Out of nowhere, another ship appeared on the horizon. Several people around Jennie gasped. No one else said a word, nor did they move. Was it chasing the opium ship? Or would it stop and rescue them? Should they keep a low profile or try to signal it?

Nate and the others were coming back slowly, scanning for floating items. They hadn't noticed the ship yet. Red Bull was still searching the wrecked captain's quarters.

Nervousness rippled through Jennie. What if this ship was full of pirates, or murderers? Or worse? She reasoned that if it was another unlawful ship, it simply wouldn't stop. She pushed away the dreadful notion that it could be another convict ship. Should they hail it?

Suddenly Fanny let out a shrill whistle. The men heard it. The women pointed toward the ship without a sound, half hoping they weren't being noticed by the approaching ship's crew. The men hastened their pace, except for Red Bull.

The wind had increased somewhat and the ship came into full view faster than the previous one. The men reached the platform and quickly began unloading their bits of retrieved items.

"It's another three-masted ship, but smaller," Nate said, once they gathered to discuss their options.

Meadows said, "The tell-tale black hull with a white strip is absent too, so it's not a clipper ship."

When it came closer Jennie noticed the prow. It had a long

bowsprit and a figurehead of a woman with arms drawn back, proudly forging ahead, her sky blue dress flowing behind her.

"Probably not an illegal ship," Meadows agreed.

"Shouldn't we be doing something to let them know we're here, then?" asked Alice.

Trust Alice to point out the obvious, thought Jennie. Her words galvanized everyone into action. They all began shouting and waving. Jennie hollered with the rest of them, admiring Alice. She was a plucky little soul and smart too.

Jennie eyed the darkening sky. The clouds were becoming more ominous, the wind gusting cooler. She wondered if they would be seen in time for the ship to stop. Would they be rescued this time?

A piercing whistle rent the air. Nate had found the bosun's pipe. He blew as hard as he could, over and over again. The shrill cheeping carried a long distance over the water. All were silent as they waited. Then there was a faint answering whistle.

The ship's sails slackened, then the ship zigzagged across the water until it seemed to be on a direct course with them. Jennie watched anxiously, a blanket of uneasiness keeping her and the others from being too certain. Then the ship was almost upon them, the name clearly emblazoned on its side: The *Lady Margaret*. Flying a Union Jack.

Jennie's heart soared. They were going to be saved.

Then came a sudden thought. She swallowed hard. If this was a British ship, would she still be subject to her conviction and sent on to Van Diemen's Land? Her thoughts dallied there for only a moment. Anything was better than perishing on the ocean. Or so she hoped.

Closer, closer the ship came. Everyone cheered.

And then it slipped past them.

An outpouring of protest charged through the group. They howled and swore. Alice whimpered, and Sarah hugged her hard. Jennie was stunned.

All at once the ship heaved to. It seemed to pause. There was a collective gasp as the ship drifted to a position several furlongs away and came to rest.

Jennie let out a breath she didn't know she'd been holding.

Within minutes a jolly boat with four men was lowered from the stern.

Jennie laughed and cried. Alice and Sarah hugged. Everyone clapped and cheered. The large platform started rocking.

"Hold still," commanded Meadows from the other side.

"Stay where you are so we are balanced. We don't want to topple now," Nate shouted.

"This will take some time, so be patient," said Meadows.

Coombs and Edwards joined the two other men. Red Bull was still a distance away, but they could see him paddling over as fast as he could.

The men talked amongst themselves. Jennie saw them gesturing and pointing, trying to figure out how to get everyone safely off the conjoined rafts without capsizing. The women babbled around her, as the jolly boat drew closer and angled next to the platform where the men stood.

An occasional word drifted over to Jennie from the conversation between the two groups of men. She gathered that the *Lady Margaret* was a merchant ship, with Scottish sailors, not British.

"That's all we bloody need. The Scots to poke at us," said Hildy quietly.

Jennie well knew the distrust and hatred that existed between the Brits and the Scots, though she didn't really understand why.

Fanny crawled over to Hildy and mumbled, "We're really between the devil and the deep sea, ain't we?"

Murmurs of agreement came from some of the women.

"Hush! Be grateful they're willing to take us aboard at all." Sarah glared at Hildy and Fanny. "We can certainly leave you behind, if you're happier with a raft."

Chastened, Hildy and Fanny clammed up. The others were subdued. Unexpectedly the men's voices rose.

"I'm staying here until everyone is on board," Meadows argued.

"As the only surviving officer, and therefore the most senior, we need you to speak to the captain of our vessel," said one of them.

Jennie watched Meadows glance around, his lips pursed grimly.

"Take me to him then," said Meadows. He assumed his responsibility with reluctant grace, giving his first order. "You're in charge of the evacuation, Nate."

Nate gave a slight nod.

Relief flooded Jennie. She certainly didn't want Red Bull in charge of anything.

Coombs started to object. Edwards stood by silently. Luckily, Red Bull was still too far off to protest against Nate, who was clearly the youngest guard and much younger than Coombs, who didn't qualify to manage the prisoners.

Meadows held up his hand. "He has proved quite capable of organizing the safe deliverance of these women. This whole operation has succeeded because of him."

He stared at Coombs. "You and Edwards are important in assisting the women to follow Nate's directions. If they do not, it will be on your head."

He turned back to Nate. "Get them loaded. Who do you want to go first?"

Nate took a deep breath and stepped forward. "We'll start with those on the outer edges on this side..."

Before he could finish speaking, a few women pushed forward, wanting to be first. The platform jiggled as they piled to the edges.

"No! Stop!" shouted Nate. "Wait your turn!"

Everyone halted.

"As each person boards the ship, the rest of you will need to shuffle to help keep the balance. I and the other men will help you do this." Nate pointed to a couple of women closest to him. "You and you, come first."

As the women stepped forward, Nate took the place of one and directed the sailors from the *Lady Margaret* to help them board the jolly boat.

He turned to Coombs. "Make your way to the other side and see that the women stay there and only move when told. Wait for my signal to have them come forward one at a time."

Nate turned to Meadows a little nervously. "Sir, if you come with me, we'll help the more severely injured women next."

Meadows nodded.

As each woman trod forward, Nate took her place. Then he switched with the next one, continuing to the centre. Meadows followed the same process. Nate relaxed a little and soon had the women shifting where he needed them.

Jennie marvelled as Nate shuffled and directed everyone, until he and Meadows reached a badly injured woman. They manoeuvred their way back with her first, much the same way they'd come. The *Lady Margaret* sailors transferred her and each of the other immobile women onto the jolly boat.

Red Bull finally pulled up to the platform, wedging his raft in close, a jubilant grin on his face. His earlier pain seemed to have left him.

With Nate's continued orchestration, the boat was soon full of the infirm. "One more space," said Nate, nodding to Meadows.

Red Bull brushed past Nate and tried to climb aboard.

"Halt!" Nate shouted, grabbing his meaty arm. "You have to wait your turn."

"There's a space and I'm here, so I'm going." Red Bull jerked away from Nate's hold.

"No, you're not." Nate leaned into his face.

"Who says?" Red Bull glared back.

Jennie could see Meadows was torn. He didn't really want to go in the first boat, but he had to. Red Bull was clearly out of line, and it was his duty to put an end to his insubordination.

"Nate says," Meadows stepped forward. "And so do I."

Two of the *Lady Margaret* sailors moved to head off Red Bull, who stopped, looking startled.

"I have a right to go first as head of the guards left. Besides, I'm injured," Red Bull pulled up his shirt to show the bandages around his middle. "I'm going."

"You have no rights at all." Meadows shoved his hands into Red Bull's chest.

Red Bull stumbled backwards onto his makeshift raft, loosely tied to the platform and was almost swamped overboard.

"You follow my orders now." Meadows glared fiercely at the burly man. "And I say wait your turn, as Nate has directed. I've given him command to manage this rescue operation." Meadows made an attempt to straighten his shirt. "And show some decency, not to mention respect in helping the others."

Red Bull glowered at Meadows. Then he gave Nate an insolent look and curled his hands into fists.

Jennie wondered if Nate was second-guessing his earlier decision to rescue the unscrupulous man.

Nate's mouth was set firmly as he stared Red Bull down. Red Bull broke eye contact first. His face full of anger, he stepped to the middle of his own small raft and turned his back on everyone. He stared toward the chunk of captain's quarters, rocking in the water some distance away.

The crew from the *Lady Margaret* pushed off with Meadows, who gave a last look of concern.

Nate began loading their own jolly boat, patiently helping and manoeuvring everyone to keep balance. Coombs and Edwards would row them. Those remaining on the platform settled in for their turn, glancing at the uncertain sky.

Jennie figured she would be among the last ones rescued with Alice and Sarah, because of their position on the platform. At least they would be together, even if the rain came soon and the crossing was miserable.

"We'll all get to go at the same time," said Sarah, echoing her thoughts.

"I'm scared." Alice hugged Sarah around her stout waist. "I don't want to go without either of you."

Jennie was scared too. What was Meadows going to say to the captain of the *Lady Margaret*? Would he tell them they were convicts and recommend they be locked up again? What kind of conditions would that mean? She barely heard Nate explaining things to the women.

"The ship is headed to South Africa to trade for salt and gold, but we're not far off from Tenerife, and they may be willing to transport us there."

"What will happen to us then?" asked Jennie. She left the rest of her questions unasked. Would the Scottish captain try to get them on another ship bound for Van Diemen's Land?

"We'll have to wait and see." Nate touched her shoulder. Jennie was transfixed by his steady gaze.

A sudden collective gasp came from behind them. Nate and Jennie spun around to look.

Across the water at the Scottish ship, an injured woman in a net halfway up the side, swung wildly over the open sea. The woman flailed and screamed. Nate took in the situation at once.

"The net's the only way they could get her up the hull with her injuries. A rope must have let go."

"Stay still!" From across the water, Jennie heard one of the *Lady Margaret* crewmen yell.

Those in the boat at the bottom shouted for the woman to stay calm. The more she flailed, the more she twirled and swung in and out against the ship.

Jennie's muscles tensed as she watched the crew strain to pull the woman up. One sailor climbed up the rope ladder and reached to grab hold of the net. He stretched too far and almost fell. Another sailor climbed down from the ship's railing. He snagged the net with a hook and pulled it in closer to the hull. The two sailors between them managed to grab the fallen rope and yard it upwards to their mates. At last the terrified woman was hauled to safety. Jennie let out a heavy sigh.

"We'll all make it," Nate said quietly beside her.

Jennie managed a small tight smile.

When the crew from the other ship returned with an extra set of oars, Nate sent Coombs and Edwards off and continued to help arrange the eldest women for the next trip. The jolly boat only held a few people at a time along with the four rowers and it was several trips before it was Jennie, Sarah and Alice's turn.

Jennie adjusted the leather medicine satchel and squeezed next to Sarah and Alice on the narrow wooden seat. Nate was the last one to get on board with them. He wedged himself onto the floor of the jolly boat between Jennie's feet. She felt his damp back against her legs and a warmth spread through her.

The wind had turned strangely still, but there were even darker clouds hovering above them. Jennie wondered when the storm would break. The sullenness of the sky merging with the granite water was oppressive, the air clammy.

"The calm before the storm," Sarah said, glancing at the sky. She held Alice closer. Jennie willed the men to row faster.

They were more than halfway to the ship, when gusts of wind whistled around them, whipping salt spray into their faces. Although the storm held off, the closer they got to the ship, the choppier the water became. Jennie looked up at the long rope ladder they had to climb. If they fell into the sea, they would be swept away.

Although Nate helped her get a firm footing on the ladder, it swayed ominously. Partway up, Jennie froze. She couldn't go back down, and her hands didn't want to pull her up. Her throat constricted. She closed her eyes.

"Keep going," Nate hollered from below.

Sarah was fast on Jennie's heels, but seemed unable to speak or move either. When Jennie looked down, Sarah gripped the rungs, white-knuckled. Jennie's heart thumped violently in her chest.

An older sailor yelled from above, "Look up here!"

Jennie riveted her eyes on the kindly faced man.

"Old Ruddick will get you up, don't you worry none." The elderly man spoke calmly in a soft Scottish lilt. "Move your hands up one at a time."

Jennie inched her hand onto the next rung and pulled, slowly lifting a foot. Her whole body swayed with the movement. She tensed and held her breath until she steadied. Resting her weight against the bow of the ship, she dared not look down again.

"Now the next one," Ruddick encouraged.

Jennie reached up with her other hand, and then lifted a foot, then another. Bit by bit she made her way to the top, keeping her focus on the wiry old sailor. At the top he leaned over and grabbed her arms, pulling her up until he caught her by the waist. Jennie was astounded by the strength in the sinewy old seaman, as he swung her over the rail and plunked her on the deck. She stood there shaking, as he reached for Sarah.

A younger sailor threw a blanket around Jennie and guided her to sit out of the wind against the bulwark with the other women. Someone else brought her water.

She clutched the cup. "Thank you," she whispered, gulping the stale, but reviving drinking water. She swished it around her mouth and let it dribble down her throat. She passed the tin cup to Sarah, as the older woman collapsed heavily against her.

One by one, the rest of the women were brought on board. Nate came up behind Alice at the last. Alice was as white as a new sail when she collapsed into Jennie and Sarah's arms.

"It was horrible. I just dangled," sobbed Alice. "The wind banged me against the ship and out again."

"There, there, my pet, you're all right now," Sarah consoled her.

Jennie imagined how difficult it would have been for Alice. The rungs were so far apart and she was such a young slip of a girl. She'd have been blown about with the wind gusts.

"Nate saved me," Alice gulped between sobs.

Jennie felt a rush of gratitude. She looked over at Nate with a blanket spread over his broad shoulders, swilling back a cup of water. He shook the sailor's hand and was guided to the captain's cabin. He pointedly ignored Red Bull standing some distance away with the other sailors, including Coombs and Edwards.

Jennie asked a passing crewman if they might have the water cup filled for Alice. When it arrived, she patted the distressed girl. "Here, Alice, drink this."

Alice gulped back her sobs and took a long drink, choking on the last of it. Jennie tapped Alice on the back until she stopped coughing, then Sarah cuddled her close.

All around them women whispered and eyed the actions on board the ship. The crew of the *Lady Margaret* seemed to be biding their time, waiting for orders. The sails were at quarter mast, flapping without any power in the wind. The ship rocked on the rough water.

Coombs and Edwards, along with Red Bull, clustered together some distance away with some of the crew of the *Lady Margaret*, waiting for orders to get underway.

Jennie heard him tell the men how, when the ship tore asunder, the quarterdeck went down first, and then the section with the captain's cabin.

"That and the mizzen and mainmast." Red Bull plied the men with tales of *his* narrow escape from death. "I did my best to hold the sails steady..."

Jennie turned away, ignoring his gravelly, bragging voice. She didn't want to listen to his lies. Nor did she want to relive the horrors of the day before. She was glad when one man broke away from the group and called for order, although he had a strange smirk on his sharp-looking face when he caught Jennie's eye.

"I am the first mate – Lieutenant Davis. The captain will address you in due course when a tactic has been decided upon for all of you. In the meantime, I'm sure you all know where the head is," he pointed forward, "and we've set up the privies for your use at any time, entering through this hatchway." He bobbed his head to his right. "That's all."

He turned to the crew and ordered, "Make fast the sails and tack the vessel!"

Being close to the hatchway, Jennie was one of the first in the queue. The wooden ladder into the hull was much the same as had been in the *Emily Anne*, though the steps were more worn with rounded edges. Candle lanterns lit their way, and even though she was among the first to use them, the privies on either side of the stern were equally soiled and foul smelling as they had been on the prisoner ship.

What amazed Jennie the most, though, was the crammed conditions of the hold with all the cargo and ship's stores packed from floor to gunwales. The pens of animals were at one end, and there was a maze through the stacked cargo to get to the privies. She stumbled and banged into kegs and crates and bales of hay and wool. She was sure a rat darted over her foot. The smell below was fetid and disgusting. She held her hand over her nose and did her business as fast as she could.

On her way back, she noticed all the hammocks for the sailors jammed together at the other end. With the sleeping quarters of the men full and the rest of the hull bursting with merchandise to be traded, Jennie wondered where the captain would put their group. At least there were only fifteen or so to be bedded down. The floor looked none too healthy.

The ship suddenly trembled and creaked, and Jennie knew they were underway. When would they find out where they were going? What had been worked out so far?

After returning topside, Jennie's thoughts focused on when they might be fed. Her body quivered with hunger. She sagged down once again beside Sarah and the sleeping Alice, who lay with her head in Sarah's lap.

"What do you think is going to happen to us now?" Jennie asked with a sense of foreboding.

Sarah met her eyes with the same haunted look, and shrugged without answering.

Jennie tucked the blanket tighter around Alice. What was their fate going to be? How long would they have to wait to learn it? She shuddered and pulled her blanket tighter.

CHAPTER SIXTEEN

JENNIE ALLOWED HER THOUGHTS to drift to her companions lost at sea. *Kate, Lizzie, Flo and Gladys.* She was saddest about Kate, of course, but Lizzie had become special to her too.

Feeling suddenly confined and needing to stretch, Jennie got to her feet and paced the deck in small circles in front of the rest of the women. When no movement by the crew was made to restrain her, she walked to the stern, leaned against the railing and gazed across the churning water.

"Get yourself over there and sit down," ordered Red Bull in Jennie's ear.

Jennie stepped back from the bully, bumping into someone behind her. She whipped around to see Meadows, glaring at Red Bull.

"This isn't our ship, Chilcott. Let her be."

For an instant Red Bull looked like he might attack Meadows, but he turned on his heels and sauntered away. Anyone else watching might have thought he had come out the winner of the confrontation, but Jennie saw the tension in his neck and knew he seethed with anger.

"Thank you," said Jennie, though fear crept up her spine. They must all watch their backs.

Meadows dipped his head, and strolled in the other direction.

Jennie turned back to the sea, leaning once again over the railing. The ship made a wide sweep around the wreckage, changing course it seemed. Lost in thought, Jennie took several moments to recognize the shape of a figure amongst the bobbing debris. It looked like a woman. The longer she looked, the more she thought she caught a glint of long copper-coloured hair.

"Sarah, come here!" she called quickly.

"What is it?" The older woman dislodged Alice and hurried to her side.

"Look over there. Just beyond that patch of wreckage. Isn't that a woman?"

"Yes, I see her!" Sarah said with excitement. By then several women had joined them.

"Maybe it's Kate." Jennie said.

"Sure could be," agreed Fanny.

Jennie called out to the crew. "There's someone still out there! We have to go back for her."

Lieutenant Davis rushed over and looked where she indicated.

"No go, lass," he said. "The way that storm is coming up, we'll be lucky to get out of its way as it is." He looked at the ominously darkening sky.

"Please, you have to try," Jennie insisted.

A great clamouring ensued between the women egging Jennie on with her repeated pleas and the first mate who continued to resist.

Nate came over. Meadows followed swiftly on his heels with the captain of the *Lady Margaret*.

"What's going on here, Lieutenant?" the captain bellowed at his first mate.

Jennie interrupted. "Please sir, there's still someone out there. We have to go back."

The captain stared where she pointed. "Hmmff. Could be anything," he said. "Whatever it is, it's not moving."

Jennie leaned over and took another look. There wasn't any movement now. "That doesn't mean she's not alive," Jennie protested.

"She?" asked the captain.

"Yes, I think it might be Kate. She's an Irish girl with red hair." Jennie kept watching.

The captain motioned to the second mate, who handed him his spyglass. He focused on the spot.

"Well?" Jennie asked.

"Could be someone," he admitted. "No way to tell if they're alive or dead from this distance." He turned to leave.

"Wait! She moved again!" Jennie pointed.

The captain focused his spyglass again. "Aye, there might be someone there."

"*Please*, sir!" Jennie begged.

Sarah joined in. "She helped save me and Alice."

"Without her we would have died," said Alice.

"We can't leave her out there if there's a chance we can rescue her," Jennie pleaded.

The captain grimaced. "All you limeys and now a bleedin' mick? I don't know what I'm going to do with the lot of you as it is – and all convicts at that."

Jennie felt her cheeks flush as the captain considered her with a cold stare. She bit the inside of her lip.

"Please, sir." She managed a thin smile. "She's my friend. She deserves a chance to be saved. She's a good person." Jennie spoke quietly, hoping she wasn't jeopardizing all of their chances at a safe haven. Nate sensed her desperation and came to her side. "I don't know how we could have missed her."

Meadows shook his head. "Hidden until the ship changed position. Or the wind may have moved her."

"I'd be up for going back," Nate said firmly. He looked at Meadows.

Meadows nodded. "Captain MacGregor, Nate and I are willing to go for her."

"But the weather, man! You'll no be able to get back safely if it breaks," Captain MacGregor objected.

"We'll use our jolly boat," said Meadows. "We won't risk any of your men."

"I'll go too, sir." Coombs stepped forward.

"Good man, Coombs," said Meadows.

Jenny looked at Red Bull. He had sauntered away and busied himself with eyeing the rigging. It was obvious he had no intention of volunteering.

"It's on your head then, Meadows."

The captain swung on his heels and stomped back toward his cabin.

"Lieutenant Davis, tell the crew to heave to. And see these men have water and food immediately." Almost as an afterthought, he added, "And get these wretches something to eat too." He waved his arm over the shipwrecked group.

Relief flooded Jennie. "Thank you, Captain MacGregor," she called after him.

"Don't make me regret it," he growled.

"Thank you too, Nate." Jennie grabbed his hand and held it in both of hers, pumping it. She turned to Meadows, bobbing her head in appreciation. "Thank you, sir."

"Let's just hope she's alive, and this isn't all for naught," he said with a wry expression. "Otherwise we've used up one of our goodwill points with the prickly Scots captain."

Jennie glanced over at Lieutenant Davis. He had a sullen look on his face. When he noticed her staring at him, he glared at her. While still keeping eye contact, he scraped his fingers under his nose, like she'd seen hooligans do in the streets back home when they didn't like someone. She had no idea what it meant, but judging from the loathing in his eyes, it couldn't be good.

Within minutes, food was distributed for the men to gobble before they left. They ate as they readied themselves, then headed for the ladder.

Jennie could hardly contain herself as the jolly boat was lowered once again and the three men got in. She knew how exhausted they were from their ordeal, and her heart swelled with gratitude. She hoped fervently that Nate came back alive with Kate.

The captain relented at the last minute and let one of his own crew – Ruddick volunteered – as the fourth rower to speed their expedition. Jennie clung to the mooring ropes on the ship's stern and watched them thrust away. She found herself praying, to whom she didn't know. She only hoped there was some greater power that would help.

At some point a piece of hardtack was shoved into her hand. Jennie nibbled on it, the chunks hitting the pit of her stomach with a thud. She'd been so long without food that her stomach wanted to reject it. Jennie managed to keep it down by accepting a cup of water and sipping at it sparingly.

Behind her, she had a vague sense of the others being fed, but she took no note, focusing entirely on the current rescue operation. After a time, Alice squeezed in next to her. The women stood nearby, shuffling occasionally for a better view.

Jennie found the salty air bracing and was thankful to be breathing it in from the safety of another ship, not still out on a raft at sea. Though what fate had planned for her, she didn't want to imagine. She and her companions were far from safe yet, especially with another tempest forming.

The wind shrilled and the wreckage rocked heavily on the open sea. As the rescuers approached the prone and immobile figure on the hunk of board, every muscle in Jennie's body tensed. There was a shared intake of breath when one of the men picked up the woman and deposited her limp body into the rowboat.

"It *is* Kate!" Alice clapped her hands.

Jennie breathed a sigh of relief.

"They got her!" The words echoed up and down the group leaning against the railing of the ship.

One step accomplished. Now for their safe return.

The captain appeared and grumbled, "One more mouth to feed *somehow!*"

The rowers stopped again when they reached their now abandoned floating platform. Jennie was amazed when they loaded some of their earlier findings into the boat. They even managed to tie the salvaged barrel behind the jolly boat before starting back again.

As they pulled vigorously on their oars, the men watched the brewing sky. Jennie could almost feel their tension as they tried to outrun the impending storm.

Before they could reach the ship, the clouds suddenly burst, and large drops of rain splattered down, pattering loudly onto the deck. Most of the women and crew on the ship ducked for cover, but Jennie stood against the starboard bulwark and let the pounding rain drench her. She was safe and alive. Sarah and Alice were safe. Kate was alive. The least she could do was stay and watch until the boat made it back.

The ship pitched in the heavy waves. Jennie's stomach lurched. But it had to be much worse for those struggling to get back. The relentless waves crashed against the small boat, flinging it about like a piece of flotsam.

Every nerve in Jennie's body tingled as she watched the rowers fight against the rolling waves that kept pushing them back. They were not far from the ship now, but for a time they lost more headway than they made.

As the boat dipped and slammed into the water, ocean spray covered them, but they persevered. Some of their salvaged items floated in the water that was gradually filling the boat. No one tried to bail. All hands were needed to keep the boat from capsizing.

"Damn fools," the captain shouted in Jennie's ear over the roar of the wind. He bellowed instructions to his men as the boat bobbed and bounced closer to the ship.

How were they going to get Kate on board in this wind? For that matter, how would the men manage it? Standing on her tiptoes, Jennie peered over the side and straight down.

The crew lowered several ropes, a hook and the net. This time it was weighted with ballast. The crew had learned from their previous encounter, and although the wind buffeted those below, they secured the net firmly with ropes and managed to use the block and tackle to their advantage. After several tries, the men in the boat snagged the net and laid Kate in it. Two men climbed onto the ladder ahead of the swinging net to steady it as best they could, keeping it drawn in with the hook, as those above heaved. Through the blinding rain, Jennie saw that Nate and Meadows had waited until the others with the net were up and secured by the sailors on deck.

The ropes were thrown down again and attached to the jolly boat. Dipping and bouncing, Nate and Meadows were able to tie a couple of ropes around the barrel. Only then did they reach for the ladder. When they were more than halfway up, the barrel was raised, followed by the winching of the boat.

Suddenly, the rain stopped, and the wind died down. It was as if someone had waved a magic wand. Everything went silent for a moment or two. Then there was a hubbub of people moving about and nattering excitedly. Convinced the two men would be safe, Jennie rushed over to where the net containing

Kate had been hoisted on board.

Jennie helped untangle Kate's limp body from the netting. Kate was breathing, but barely. There was a large gash on the back of her head. No longer bleeding, and freshly washed by the rain, it was still a nasty gouge. She also had other cuts and scrapes on her body. "Kate." Jennie gently shook her, but she didn't respond.

"She's been coshed by something, I'd say," said a Scottish sailor, leaning over Kate.

"Let's hope she'll come around," said Sarah tenderly.

The captain pushed through the surrounding crowd. He surveyed the scene and ordered Kate taken under a shelter near the bulwark in the waist of the ship.

"This girl goes with her." He pointed to Jennie. "The rest of you stay back."

"Cabin boy!" Captain MacGregor called.

A young lad stepped forward. "Aye, sir!"

"You are to get them what they need." The captain started to head off.

"Can I help too?" asked Alice, stepping forward. "I've helped with injured people before."

Captain MacGregor raised his eyebrows in disbelief, then he sighed. "How two chits of girls can do doctoring is beyond me." He paused, seeming to make up his mind. "Go on with you, lass." He gave Alice a wave of dismissal.

Clutching her leather pouch, Jennie hurried after the sailors carrying Kate. Alice stuck close behind her and the cabin boy brought up the rear. The sailors laid Kate on a blanket in a dry spot of the deck under a scrap of tarp that had been strung up for them.

"Fetch a cloth and water, please," Jennie said, sinking to her knees.

The cabin boy obliged, and Alice gently towelled Kate off, while Jennie tended to the gash in her head, tenderly picking her red curly hair from the wound.

"Is there no surgeon?" Jennie asked the cabin boy standing over her. He looked very young, maybe not much older than Alice.

"The doctor died a week back." He shrugged.

Jennie groaned inwardly. "Right, then. Ah...what's your name?"

"Angus, miss," he said.

"Well, then, Angus...where's the surgery? We need to sew her up."

"We don't rightly have one of those either, miss," he said.

"No surgery?" Jennie's voice came out sharp with surprise.

Angus shook his head. "The surgery, or wardroom as we calls it, is used for, well, other things. The doctor had a berth where he kept his medical satchel...but he did most of his work in the galley."

"Where the food is cooked?" Jennie was incredulous.

"Nowhere else to rightly do things, miss," he sputtered, his face turning a bright shade of red. "That's where the knives and saws are for amputations and such."

He spoke as if amputating a limb was an everyday occurrence, and doing it where they prepared their meals was a sensible thing to do. She was glad they'd been fed hardtack and not soup.

Jennie looked around at the rough nature of the ship. Deck boards were polished but worn, cleats and other equipment showed signs of rust. From the looks of the sails, they'd been mended many times, and the masts looked none too sturdy. Maybe it wasn't so surprising that the surgery was in the galley, and there was so much need to sever limbs. They no doubt had plenty of accidents.

"The captain has medicine supplies in his cabin," Angus offered.

Jennie nodded. Out of the corner of her eye, she saw Nate

and Meadows return on board. Nate stumbled and fell as he skidded onto the wet deck. Meadows collapsed beside him, breathing hard, but smiling. They shook hands and grinned triumphantly.

"We did it," said Nate. Coombs joined them, and they slapped each other on the back.

They had *rescued* Kate. Now it was Jennie's turn to *save* her.

She focused her attention back to her unmoving friend, as sailors welcomed the men with blankets and shots of rum. Jennie continued to check Kate for more injuries, testing for broken bones. She found only scrapes and cuts.

Jennie sat back on her heels and unfastened her leather pouch. She set out the little tins. All of them were miraculously safe and dry, if somewhat dented. Opening each, she examined their contents. Besides the dried yarrow flowers and lard, she'd grabbed some pulverized marigolds. She'd make a poultice. At least that would keep the swelling down on Kate's head. She had no idea what else to do.

"We need a bowl with warm water and another cloth for washing, and a bowl for mixing a plaster and strips for bandages. Oh, and a needle and something for sutures." She rattled off the list with authority.

"I don't rightly know where to find some of those things," he said. "I'll speak to the captain for you, miss."

"Well, quickly, then."

"And a spoon too," added Alice.

"Right you are," said Jennie, winking at her smart young friend. She'd forgotten to mention the spoon for mixing the poultice.

Alice grinned and called after the cabin boy, "The cook will have the spoon and bowls."

Jennie added, "And he should have some water already on the hob too."

The girls set back to work.

After a time, Alice said, "I don't think Angus is much older than me."

"I'm sure you're right," Jennie replied.

Alice had a quizzical expression on her face. "Why would he be working on a ship so young?"

"I don't know, but you could ask him. Here he comes."

Alice blushed, and dropped her head as Angus returned.

"Captain MacGregor says you're to join him in his cabin and select what you need."

"All right," said Jennie, rising. Angus stayed behind with Alice.

The storm clouds had dissipated, but the afternoon wore on and the sky dimmed as the sun failed. She'd have to hurry to sew Kate up before dark. She didn't fancy doing anything by candlelight.

When she arrived outside the captain's quarters, she looked around. Neither the first mate nor anyone else was there to let the captain know she'd arrived. With trepidation, Jennie tapped lightly on the thick oak cabin door, not sure what she'd find when she entered.

CHAPTER SEVENTEEN

"ENTER," CAPTAIN MACGREGOR bade Jennie.

She opened the door and stepped over the threshold into his cramped quarters. The captain sat at an oak table, writing in a book with thick wooden covers. Beside him was a squat bottle of black ink, a pen holder and two leather-bound books. One was open and had a list of scribbles with a column of numbers beside them. Nearby was a large mug holding amber liquid. A rectangular table jammed against the opposite wall held several charts, along with a compass, sextant and a large hourglass mounted on a three-legged stand.

Behind the captain there was a bed. Jennie blushed at the impropriety of being in a man's sleeping chambers. She looked away quickly.

"I understand you are in need of surgical supplies," said the captain, not unkindly.

"Yes, sir," she said, glancing up at him, then quickly at the floor.

"You can look at me, my dear," he said, taking a draught from his mug.

She raised her eyes to his amused ones. His face was rugged and a bit weathered. His smile reminded her of her father's and she relaxed a little.

"That's better." He swept his hand toward a closed cabinet. "There is where you'll probably find what you require. Take what you need."

"Yes, sir," she said, inspecting the collection of apothecary items and medical instruments.

Within moments she'd spied the needle and suturing materials. She selected some and draped bandage strips over her forearm. As she did so, her eyes fastened on a small, intricately designed wooden box about the size of a thick Bible, just above the supply shelf. She glanced over at the captain. He was still engaged with his work.

She ran her hand over the carved box momentarily, then dropped her hand. The box had a tiny keyhole with key. Her father had crafted a trinket box like it for her mother's scant bit of jewellery and locks of hair from all her children. Her mother had added a curl from her husband's fair head after he'd died. Jennie thought longingly of her family.

"Anything else then?" the captain asked, peering at her.

She started guiltily and showed him what she'd chosen. "All I need now are the bowls, the spoon and hot water," she answered.

"Yes, yes," he said, impatiently draining the contents of his mug. "The cabin boy will have those for you shortly." He wiped his arm across his mouth and turned back to his writing. "Bring back what you don't use, please, lass, even if I'm not here."

"I will. Thank you, sir," she said, dipping into a little curtsy. "And thank you too, for rescuing Kate."

"We'll see how you do with stitching her and making her well," he said. He scribbled for a moment, then paused with his pen and gave her a swift glance. "For a young girl, not to mention an English one at that, you may be worth your salt, after all."

"I hope so sir," she said. She waited for him to speak again, but he'd already gone back to his entries.

"Were the things from the rafts useful, sir?" she dared to ask.

"I'm unaware of such as you speak. I haven't seen anything yet." He scowled into his papers, his shaggy hair falling into his eyes. "But I'm sure time will tell."

As she scurried out of the cabin and closed the door, Jennie blew out a breath of embarrassment. She hadn't seen the salvaged items either, but she hoped they were useful, since she'd spouted off to the captain in an effort to make herself and her companions look worthy. For all she knew, everything the men had found was only good for the rubbish bin.

Except for maybe what Red Bull had stashed away. As she hurried back to Kate and Alice, her mind flicked over the red-headed brute stuffing his pockets. She scowled, determined to find out what he'd taken. But where had he hidden it?

All at once, Nate fell into step with her.

"Something amiss?" he asked.

Jennie was taken aback for a moment, but here was her chance to tell Nate what she suspected about Red Bull.

"A bit." She glanced about. Red Bull was deep in conversation with Davis down the deck by the jolly boat. No one else lingered nearby.

"Well, I'm not sure exactly, but I thought you should know, even though it may mean nothing." A breath caught in her throat.

"Go on." His gentle smile dazzled her. She found herself tongue-tied for a moment. But she recovered and told him of Red Bull's actions while searching the wreckage. When she was done, Nate flicked a speculative glance toward Red Bull. Jennie felt apprehensive.

"Probably making off with something valuable," Nate agreed. "I'll see what I can find out and handle it," he said, heading off without another word in the direction of Red Bull. Jennie groaned. She hadn't wanted Nate to confront Red Bull, only to keep watch.

Jennie rushed back to Kate and Alice. Alice sat next to a steaming bowl of water, swabbing Kate's body sores. Kate was still unresponsive. Jennie knelt to begin making the poultice. She and Alice worked quietly together for a time, and then Alice began whistling softly. Jennie started humming to the tune to help pass the time, and was soon whistling along.

Suddenly, Davis was before them, shouting. "Halt your whistling, you heathen lasses! Don't you bleeding well know not to whistle on a ship?"

Stunned to silence, Alice froze. Jennie stopped drawing a suture mid-stitch.

He bent right into their faces and cursed at them. Spittle flew from the first mate's mouth as he yelled. Sailors nearby crossed themselves.

Meadows and Nate hurried over from where they'd been speaking with Red Bull.

"They're sorry, Lieutenant." Meadows guided the officer by the shoulder away from Jennie and Alice. "They *didn't* know any better. But now they *do*. I'll make sure it doesn't happen again."

Davis brushed Meadow's hand off roughly. "See that it doesn't," he snarled, clenching his fists. "We don't need you barmy bunch of English halfwits invoking another adverse wind," he railed on. "We don't need no more harm to the ship or to the crew."

"Lieutenant Davis, stand down." Captain MacGregor said calmly, appearing at his side.

The lieutenant flashed a glance of reproach at the captain, a menacing glare at Jennie and Alice and a look of hatred at Nate. Then he stomped off. The captain glowered at the rest of his crew, and they scuttled back to their tasks.

Tears had formed in Alice's eyes. Jennie hugged her, saying, "It's all right. I don't know why whistling is bad, but we didn't mean any harm."

Nate crouched beside them. "Tradition is that you must never whistle on a ship for fear it brings bad luck," he explained, as if he was trying hard not to sound too exasperated. "Seems they've been having nothing but bad luck their whole trip out."

He nodded to Angus. "Isn't that right?"

Angus shrugged and departed.

"But why do they think that about whistling?" asked Jennie.

"It's what all sailors believe – a longstanding superstition that whistling on a ship will summon gale force winds," Nate said.

Alice gulped. "I won't ever do it again."

"I'm sure you won't," Nate said, patting her head. "Whistling women and crowing hens are neither fit for God nor men." Nate quoted a saying Jennie hadn't heard before. "They're already feeling jumpy with all you women on board – also considered a bad omen."

"What about the bosun's whistle then?" Alice asked shyly.

"That's not the same as a person whistling a tune," Nate explained. "It's actually a pipe used to give commands because its high pitch can be heard over the sounds of the sea and bad weather."

Alice thought about it for a minute. "And for emergencies like when we needed to be rescued."

"Indeed."

She gave Nate a brief smile and turned back to spread the poultice on Kate's injuries.

Jennie stood to face him. "Do you believe it?"

He gave her a puzzled expression. "What? About crowing hens, or whistling women?"

Jennie frowned. "No, about whistling on a ship bringing bad luck."

"Maybe I would if I were a sailor." He shrugged and walked away.

As she turned back to nursing Kate, Jennie mulled their

conversation over, but couldn't really make any sense of Nate's answer. True, he worked as a guard, but he definitely had the ability to work on water.

At last, satisfied she'd done all she could for her friend, Jennie headed to the captain's cabin to return the unused supplies.

The heavy door was open when she arrived. She knocked tentatively, but there was no response. She stepped inside quickly and deposited the supplies back on the shelf below the small, carved box. With a quick glance, she noted the captain had removed the key. Stepping back outside, she saw him walking back to his cabin and dipped her head in thanks. At the same time, Nate passed her with a smile.

"Wait," Jennie called after him.

He stopped mid-stride.

"Can I ask you something?" Jennie looked around to see if anyone else was listening. "In private."

He raised an eyebrow.

"Do you know where we're going for sure?" she asked.

"To Tenerife," he said.

"That is good news." Jennie felt relieved to know at least that much had been decided.

"I think the captain has had enough of whistling and of women," said Nate with a teasing lilt to his voice. "He doesn't want to keep any of us any longer than he has to, and southern Africa would be too far."

Jennie grimaced and felt the heat rise in her face. "Do you know what happens to us after that?"

Nate shook his head. "It may depend on what ships are there when we arrive."

"Can you tell me what the captain knows about us?"

"He knows you're all convicts, if that's what you mean."

Jennie had already known that, but still it was hard to hear it from Nate's lips. What must he think of her?

"Will he put us on another convict ship for Van Diemen's Land, do you think, or maybe send us back to jail in England?"

"The captain hasn't decided yet, and it could take some time to learn what ships are en route." Nate's eyes showed compassion. "I'm sorry I can't tell you more."

Jennie couldn't say anything, as Nate looked at her steadily. Her mouth didn't seem to work.

"He knows his duty," Nate added gently.

Jennie dropped her chin to her chest and fiddled with the cloth in her hand.

Nate added, "But he's also not overly fond of us Brits and would like to stick it to us, including our legal system, apparently."

Her head bounced back up. Maybe there was a spark of hope. Then she recalled that Scottish and British people had similar laws.

Nate answered her question without her asking. "Anything to thwart English legal authorities, I'd guess." He had a grim smile. "Though he wouldn't want to lose his commission. I don't know what the outcome will be."

"What did Meadows say?"

"Meadows is a fair man, but it's naught to do with him. It's Captain MacGregor's responsibility to work out with the authorities." He looked out to sea.

Jennie twisted the cloth in her hands. Did she dare ask Nate how he personally felt?

Before she could ask, Nate said, "Meadows and I spoke to Chilcott – your Red Bull – about what you saw on the rafts."

"And?" Jennie sucked in her breath.

"He denied finding or hiding anything he hasn't shared."

Jennie scowled. "He would then, wouldn't he? I know he took something for himself."

"Chilcott offered to let Meadows search him, but it was plain he had nothing hidden on him." Nate shrugged. "We'll have to let it go."

Jennie heaved a sigh.

"At least for now," Nate added.

She glanced around to locate Red Bull. He and some sailors were moving barrels and crates from the jolly boat to the area around the mainmast.

"Now he'll have it in even worse for me."

She wished Meadows and Nate hadn't said anything to Red Bull, just somehow caught him, instead. She was sure Red Bull had been doing what he ought not to be.

Nate touched her shoulder.

"We said *we'd* seen him, but watch yourself, Jennie," he warned. "I think he suspects you're the one who saw him."

"What did he say?"

Nate shrugged with a mild shake to his head. "Nothing you want to hear. But he did accuse you of spying on him in his usual unpleasant way. He may retaliate."

Jennie nodded solemnly. "I'll be careful."

"Good. He's a cruel bastard. We'll all have to watch our backs." Nate squeezed her shoulder and was gone.

Jennie stood for some moments, feeling the warmth on her shoulder where Nate's hand had been and contemplating how to stay out of Red Bull's way.

"Jennie, look!" Alice called. "Kate's stirring."

Jennie rushed back. Bewildered, the Irish girl looked at Jennie and Alice. Jennie dropped down beside her. "Kate. Oh, I'm so glad to see you've come awake."

"What's happened?" she asked.

"We've been shipwrecked," Alice said. "Don't you remember?"

She groaned. "Ooh, my head. It hurts something fearful."

"You've been coshed," Alice explained.

Kate tried to lift her arm and groaned again. "It won't move.

I have no use of my limb," she fretted.

"It's all right, Kate. You're hurt, and you need to rest." Jennie eased her back down.

"You must lie still," said Alice, softly stroking Kate's forehead.

"But where are we?" she repeated. The fear had not left her eyes.

"We've been rescued by another ship, the *Lady Margaret*," Jennie said.

Alice leaned in to tell Kate about their rescue. Nate passed by and touched Jennie lightly on the shoulder.

"You did well with Kate. See you later." He headed in Meadows' direction.

A feeling Jennie couldn't identify spread through her like a warm tide. She hugged the feeling to herself.

Not long after, the captain appeared, carrying his tin drinking mug. He walked unsteadily and his face was flushed.

When he spied Lieutenant Davis deep in conversation with Red Bull, he bellowed, "Lieutenant, get these people moved into the hold. Though God in heaven only knows where you'll put them. This is a merchant vessel, not a bleeding passenger ship." He belched and made his way to starboard, where he leaned heavily against the bulwark.

Jennie didn't know where everyone would go either, but she was surprised by the captain's sudden change in demeanour. She wondered if Captain MacGregor had fallen ill, or he was overwrought with concern over something more than not having enough food or space for everyone.

There were about eighteen people from the shipwreck with the crew, guards and women. The injured with the broken arms and legs would have to stay above board.

Would she have to ask Captain MacGregor's permission to stay on deck with them? She could say she needed Alice and

Sarah to help her. Jennie hoped he'd let them stay above board, especially if the weather held. She didn't want to be crammed into the dark stench of the hold, lying on the floor with the rats, under the smelly men in hammocks. And she did not want to be anywhere near Red Bull.

So far the evening was mild and the ocean calm. A pastel pink sunset floated on the horizon. She'd never been allowed to stay on deck this late before. And here she was without any restraints. It was almost like being on that exotic voyage she'd imagined so many times while trudging in endless circles on the deck of the *Emily Anne*.

"Oooh, my head is swimming. I feel like I'm going to heave." Kate was trying to sit up, aided by Alice, who held a basin under her chin.

"Breathe through your nose, Kate," said Jennie, dropping back down beside her. She turned to Alice. "Would you mind getting some drinking water for her?"

Alice jumped to her feet and went in search of Angus.

As soon as Alice was gone, Jennie made sure Kate was comfortable, then said, "Lie still. I'll be right back."

She approached the captain, still leaning against the bulwark with his elbows on the railing. His eyes were closed and he breathed heavily, hands propping up his chin.

"Captain McGregor," she said softly.

He let out a snort. His eyes popped open. He blinked and leaned toward her. "Just taking in the night air, lass." His words came out slurred.

Jennie recoiled. The man reeked of rum. She stared at him with her mouth open. When he tilted his head, she could see his bloodshot eyes and his red nose. He reminded her of her family's drunken landlord. This was obviously not a good time to ask for any favours.

"I'm going to my quarters now." He took another drink and

swayed, sloshing some liquid from his cup. As he passed her, he stumbled.

"Uh, do you want some help, sir?" she asked.

"Certainly not." His empty mug dangled loosely from his fingers. Jennie caught it when it fell and handed it back to him. He wobbled off, listing to one side all the way to his quarters.

"What's wrong with him?" asked Alice, joining her.

"Too much rum." Jennie turned toward the bulwark to hide her shock. She'd hoped the captain would be someone she might count on, someone who might help them.

"Are you all right?" asked Alice. She peeked at Jennie's face.

"What's this all about then?" asked Sarah, coming up to them.

"Our new captain is a drunk," Jennie whispered to them.

Sarah's eyes opened wide. "Lord love a duck, what next?"

Jennie realized that must be why Captain MacGregor's ship was in such a state of disrepair and the crew was in disarray. It was probably also why Davis had such a superior air, more like that of a bull – Red Bull. The captain was probably drunk most of the time.

She straightened as she saw Davis, Meadows and Nate coming their way. Red Bull trailed nonchalantly behind at a distance. The captain's drunkenness might not bode well for any of them, if Davis was in charge while his master slept.

"What's the status of the injured woman?" asked Lieutenant Davis, stepping right up to Jennie.

"She's awake, but in pain. She'll live," Jennie replied, staring boldly at Davis.

"The captain will be pleased," said Davis, giving her a wry, almost sarcastic smile.

Behind him Red Bull scowled.

"Well done," Meadows said.

"She can't be moved though, sir," Jennie added to Davis.

He nodded. "She'll stay deckside tonight, then. And you with her." He stated it as a fact not a request.

Jennie agreed, grateful not to have to argue for it. Alice looked at her wistfully. "It would be good if Alice could stay as well, sir," she said, crossing her fingers behind her back.

"You may have her with you," he answered. "And you?" He turned to Sarah. "I suppose you'd like to remain with your daughters?"

Sarah didn't correct him. Instead, she bobbed, "Well, yes, of course, if I may. Yes, sir, thank you." She clasped her hands in front of her.

Jennie slid a sideways glance at Sarah and Alice, then at Nate. He rolled his eyes at them behind the lieutenant's back, but didn't say anything. Surprisingly, Meadows didn't either.

"We already have the women with the broken bones up here too. You will be responsible for them as well as any others who are not able to get down the ladder on their own." Davis looked at them gravely, as if daring them to protest. "There isn't anywhere to put them in the hold in any regard."

Jennie nodded. "I understand, sir. We will take good care of them."

"Right then. We'll hope the weather holds."

"Perhaps you'd be good enough to allow myself and my man here," Meadows indicated Nate, "to also stay on deck."

"I'm sure you'll be quite comfortable in the stern," said Davis.

Red Bull made a movement as if to request the same, but Meadows pretended not to see. "My other men will go below deck to keep watch over the women."

Red Bull's face suffused with scarlet. Jennie watched him clench his fists at his side. Coombs didn't look happy either, but he didn't protest, nor did Edwards.

A frown creased Davis' forehead for an instant, and his eyes turned cold. "I can assure you, my crew can take care of the women below. Your men will find more room on deck."

Meadows acquiesced. "As you wish."

Red Bull's demeanour cheered considerably.

Davis continued with a frosty scoff. "How we'll feed you all in the morning is another problem. We're two days – three days maximum – out of Tenerife by my calculations, so we'll have to manage somehow."

Jennie knew that feeding them all had been one of the things the captain had worried about. But this didn't make sense to her. Why were they so short of food? Surely, if Tenerife hadn't been a planned stop, they would have more stored on board for a long voyage. Why were they in such dire straits? Or was there something more sinister afoot?

"Have you not seen the stores we've brought from the rafts then?" Meadows inquired.

Davis looked mystified. "All I saw was the barrel of wet gunpowder and a few odds and ends of broken ship gear."

Nate motioned toward the jolly boat. Jennie looked to where the crew had turned it upside down after stacking its contents against the mainmast railing some distance away. "Those crates and barrels hold salt pork and oatmeal and other food."

Davis stared hard at Red Bull. "I was not made aware of these provisions."

Red Bull looked away.

Jennie was pleased they had found something useful to share with the Scottish crew. But when had Nate and the others found the food? Had they been holding it back like she worried they might? But there wasn't anywhere they could have hidden it. Then she recalled the men hurrying back when the *Lady Margaret* suddenly arrived. They hadn't had time to unload their finds. They must have brought it to the ship when they rescued Kate. Hopefully the food contribution would put them in a favourable position with the captain. Red Bull's reluctance to mention it to Davis was curious, however. She thought the two of them had seemed quite chummy.

Jennie glanced at the sky. Dusk had fallen quickly with twilight bringing out a dusting of stars and a slit of golden moon suspended just above the calm glistening waters that stretched to the horizon. The rest of the women called out good night as they descended into the belly of the ship. Fanny was the last to file past. She grinned at Jennie as Iris began reciting her evening prayers even louder than usual.

A few minutes later Angus appeared with some dry blankets. They smelled of must and other things Jennie didn't want to think about.

"Would you have something for Kate to nibble on too?" she asked. "She hasn't eaten anything yet."

Angus nodded and disappeared down the hatch. Sarah and Alice spread out the extra blankets on either side of Jennie. The men carried over the woman with the broken limbs and laid her on Kate's right side. Then the others limped over.

"Ooh, I'm so grateful to be with the lot of you," said the elderly woman, grimacing with pain as she eased herself down. "Name's Mary."

"Which Mary are you?" Jennie smiled, as she helped Kate sit up so she could eat the biscuit Angus brought her.

"Mary Breck," she said. She added in a breathless rush, "But you can call me May if you like. That's what my mate used to call me, on account he had a sister and mother called Mary already, bless his soul."

Jennie had seen May around, of course, but hadn't come to know her.

The odd gust of cool wind ruffled over them, but once Jennie snuggled next to Alice, she warmed up. Above them, Nate checked the tightness of the ropes on the tarp strung over their heads.

"It will hold as long as we don't get any strong winds," he said, frowning at a slightly frayed rope.

"Thanks, Nate," said Jennie.

"Good night," he grunted.

"Good night to you too," said Jennie with a soft sigh.

Alice was already asleep. The others seemed to be dozing. Near the bow, Jennie heard the murmur of men's voices and clinking of cups, then an occasional laugh. She recognized Red Bull's harsh accent, Davis' gruff guttural voice and Meadows' voice too. After a time, she heard someone stumble off, and then there was silence.

As the night settled down around them, Jennie gazed at the stars, bright pinpricks in the dark, velvet sky. They reminded her of home and her life, so, so long ago. She wiped away the dampness on her cheek and folded away her memories. Closing her eyes, she wondered what the new day would bring.

CHAPTER EIGHTEEN

"BLOODY HELL! There's a thief in our midst!"

The captain's roar woke Jennie with a start. She'd been in a deep sleep, the best she'd had for weeks. The women around her might have fared the same, judging by their slowness to wake. It was hardly daybreak.

The crew on watch looked startled and busied themselves with the rigging and sails. Red Bull was among them, restacking the goods they'd brought from the rafts. He stole glances at Captain McGregor, rampaging from the doorway of his quarters.

"Thieving Brits!" The captain bellowed and called for his lieutenant.

Davis appeared from his berth, still buttoning his tunic. He made his way to the captain. MacGregor yanked him inside, cursing and yelling something that sounded like "Madmen, Englishmen and damned thieves," as he slammed the door.

Davis appeared outside again moments later.

"Meadows!" he shouted.

Meadows quickly approached. Off to the side, Nate stood looking alert though his hair was unkempt. He hurriedly tucked in his crumpled shirt and followed Meadows.

Alice clutched Jennie's arm. "What is it? What's happened?"

She blinked sleep from her eyes.

Sarah lay tense beside them; Kate and May were wide-eyed and watchful.

"I don't know," Jennie whispered. "Shh!"

"One of your thieving charges stole the captain's gold coins," Davis spat out.

In shock, Meadows looked at Nate, and then back to Davis. "But none of them had access to the captain's quarters. They wouldn't even know he had coins, or where they were kept."

"Think again," Davis spat, glancing pointedly toward Jennie's group.

Jennie gulped. She was the only one who had been in the captain's quarters. But there must be some mistake.

A slow flush crept up Meadows' neck.

"Yes, that thieving girl." Davis glowered.

"But she wouldn't have!" Nate protested, stepping forward.

"She did go into the captain's quarters," said Meadows quietly.

"But only for the medical supplies," Nate stated.

Jennie leapt up to defend herself. "I was in the captain's quarters, but he invited me in and he was there the whole time!"

"Time enough for you to case the place and sneak back later." Davis glared at her.

"Why would I do that?" Jennie gritted her teeth.

"The obvious reasons," Davis said coldly.

"But I didn't!" she protested again. She felt Sarah and Alice's presence next to her. Out of the corner of her eye, she saw Red Bull edging closer.

"Isn't it true you did go back later in the afternoon when the captain wasn't in his cabin? I saw you myself," Davis accused, his eyes glowering.

"Well, yes, to return the needle and suturing materials. But he told me to," she retorted, her pulse racing. "He saw me go in."

"Long enough to take something?" Davis continued his grilling.

"No! I didn't. I swear! I was only in for a few seconds." Her palms were sweating. "I left the door open."

"Just time enough time to take the key?" Davis said with disdain.

"The key wasn't in the box!" she snapped again.

"Ah-ha so you admit you saw the box and knew about the key," he challenged.

"Of course, I saw the box," she said indignantly. "It was right in front of my eyes above the surgical supplies. I couldn't help but notice it. My father made my mother one just like it."

Nate stepped forward. "I saw her too. She was in and out... no time for anything."

"*That* time," said Davis.

"When else could she have done it?" Nate asked.

"During the night."

"But she was asleep beside us all night." Sarah stepped up. "I'd have taken notice."

"And were you awake *all* night to *know* if she was there the *whole* time?" asked Davis rudely, punctuating key words.

"Well, no." Sarah drooped. She squeezed Jennie's hand.

"Or are the pair of you maybe covering up for her?" Davis accused.

"Of course not." Sarah and Alice shuffled back a step.

Meadows and Nate considered the circumstances without saying a word. Red Bull slipped in closer with an odd, expectant look on his face. Jennie went into shock. Her mind whirled with the unfairness of Davis' accusations and his attacks on her integrity. Suddenly, she felt anger rising in her.

"I was caring for Kate all afternoon and evening, and then I went straight to sleep," she said through gritted teeth. "I never went to the captain's quarters without his permission."

"Not quite," Davis peered around at all those nearby, as if giving a grand denouement in Old Bailey. "At some point in the night you rose and returned to Captain MacGregor's quarters and wilfully stole from him."

"No, I didn't!" Jennie countered. "How would I have known where the key was? It wasn't there when I went back the second time."

"Ahh, so how did you know that the gold coins were in the box?" He raised his eyebrows at her. "I never said where the coins were kept." He smirked at the others.

"I *didn't* know they were kept there," she snapped. "I'm not a simpleton. You're the one quizzing me about the box and key; it's not hard to figure it out," she said indignantly, jamming her hands onto her hips.

"Look, here," said Meadows. "She does have a point."

"She wouldn't have done something like that, I'm sure." The look on Nate's face said he believed her, but Jennie knew Davis had planted a seed of doubt.

"Easy to believe, if she weren't already a convicted thief," Davis said. He stared down his nose at her.

"I'm not a common thief, but I do have eyes in my head like everyone else!" she retorted. How dare he accuse her of stealing the coins!

"Ah, but isn't that why you're here? For thievery?" Davis looked smug.

Jennie felt her face go hot.

"But that was different," she said in a low voice.

"How? You stole something that didn't belong to you!"

"It was a mouldy sack of oats, and in a rubbish bin! Not something anyone wanted!" she spat out.

"Still, it wasn't yours!" Davis punched a fist into his other hand with a loud smack. He leaned forward, looking hard into her eyes.

Nate moved as if to come to her aid, but Meadows put a restraining arm on his elbow.

Gathering his composure, Davis straightened. "So, we're back to you sneaking in during the night then, if we are to believe you didn't take the coins when the captain knew you were there."

Jennie mutely shook her head.

"The captain would have heard someone entering his quarters in the middle of the night," Nate protested.

Davis gave him a withering look. "The captain was as drunk as a lord. Like usual. He wouldn't have noticed if someone had robbed the clothes off his very person."

Red Bull snickered. Jennie threw him a sharp look. He grinned openly at her, no longer pretending he was doing anything but paying attention to the exchange and pleased at her discomfort.

"Others would have heard someone creeping about the deck," Nate pushed in.

"Did you?" Davis gave him another smirk. "I rather think you were all in your cups too." He glanced swiftly at Nate and Meadows. "And we already know the madam and the child weren't awake to see anything."

Meadows shook his head at Nate, warning him to keep out of it. Nate ignored him and stepped between Jennie and Davis.

"You can't just accuse her of doing this because she happens to have been in the captain's quarters earlier and saw the box. You said yourself..." Meadows grabbed Nate's arm, but he shook him off. "You said the captain was drunk, so *anyone* could have gone in."

"But not just *anyone* did, did they? She's the only one who knew about the box." Davis shook his fingers into Nate's face.

Jennie was grateful for Nate's support, but the whole thing had gone on long enough. Many of the women, who had since been released on deck, and some of the crew had gathered into a crowd just beyond them.

"I didn't steal anything." She pushed in front of Nate. "I'd have nowhere to stow it, would I?" She whirled around in her tattered shift that showed the form of her body and obviously no place to hide anything.

"Oh, I'm sure you hid it. Maybe on one of your friends." Davis seemed to be toying with her. He smiled. "How about we search all of you?"

"You already know you won't find anything." Jennie crossed her arms over her chest.

She glanced at Sarah and Alice. They both did a slow full turn with their arms lifted to their sides, then came to stand beside Jennie.

"I think you'd have hidden it better than that anyway," said Davis, shoving past her.

He strode over to Kate and Mary, and made a show of flinging the blankets about.

Jennie and the others rushed after him.

Almost instantly he pounced on the leather pouch that contained the medicines.

"Don't," Jennie shouted as he dumped it upside down. "You'll spill all the medicines." But it was too late. Everything clattered onto the deck in a heap: dried flowers, tins, lids, lard – and a number of gold coins.

Jennie heard a collective gasp. The women closest to her had gone pale.

"What? I don't understand!" She gaped at the coins on the floor of the deck. Where had they come from? "I didn't put them in there. Honestly, I didn't."

But the look in everyone's eyes told her they no longer believed she was innocent. Even Nate gave her a peculiar look. Alice and Sarah stood stock still, eyes frozen.

Then all at once chattering and arguing erupted. Sarah and Alice were the first to defend her innocence, and soon the other women protested at her unfair accusers. The sailors hooted and hollered for her blood.

In the ensuing mêlée, Jennie watched one gold piece roll across the deck as if in slow motion, unnoticed by the others. Red Bull stopped it with his foot. Snatching it into his burly hands with glee, he glanced around and slid it into his shirt.

Before she knew what was happening, Meadows seized her arm.

"No wait! I don't know how those coins got there!" Jennie protested, but no one tried to save her. "Someone must have put them there."

She looked frantically at Nate. He gave her a negligible shrug of helplessness. His eyes told her nothing.

Davis put a hand on Meadows' forearm. "She's on board my ship, and I give the orders, so *we'll* deal with her."

"She's one of my charges," argued Meadows. "I'll mete out justice to her."

"Hand her over to me," Davis ordered, his voice hardening.

"I'll take her for you, sir," said Red Bull. It wasn't clear which man he was calling sir. He rushed over and grabbed Jennie's arm.

Jennie jerked to get away, but Red Bull held on tight. She kicked hard, connecting with his upper thigh, missing her central target. He let go with a snarl.

Davis turned on Red Bull and hissed, "I told you I'd take care of her!"

Jennie raised her eyes. What was this power struggle about?

With attention diverted, Meadows grabbed Jennie's other arm and dragged her a short distance away.

"Please, sir," she begged. "I didn't steal the coins. I don't know how they got there."

"Stop thrashing about," he ordered. "We'll get to the bottom of this."

She halted. "You mean you believe me?"

Meadows shook his head, still with a firm grip on her arm. "Not exactly, but I do believe in investigating more fully before we make a decision." He tilted his head toward the coins. "So far it looks damning."

Jennie searched his face, but his eyes were cold, his manner aloof.

"Someone else must have put them there," she said, quieter now.

"We'll see." He didn't seem thoroughly convinced. "I have no jurisdiction on board this ship and the Lieutenant will bring the captain in a minute, so you'd best go with him."

"Please don't let Red Bull take me," begged Jennie.

He shook his head and grimaced. "At least *he* will have to follow my orders." His manner softened somewhat. "Now come along." He pushed Jennie firmly forward between her shoulder blades.

Although Jennie went back meekly to Davis, fear seized her. What did they do to thieves on this ship?

Red Bull openly snickered at her as she passed him. She leaned and spat on him. He raised a fist as if to strike her, but Nate caught his hand.

"Please, you have to believe me. I didn't steal the coins!" She looked with beseeching eyes at Nate. "It had to be someone else!"

His gaze seemed distant. She glanced over her shoulder at Sarah and Alice. The young girl stood still watching everything, her face contorted as if she was about to howl. Sarah looked at her steadily with a troubled expression.

Davis took her below deck himself, motioning for Old Ruddick to light a lantern quickly and come along. Jennie's heart thumped. What was going to become of her now? Any hopes of getting a reduced sentence or a reprieve through some miracle were definitely gone.

Davis roughly pushed her through the hatchway and down the uneven steps of the ladder. Old Ruddick had gone first with the lantern, but no light was cast her way, and she stumbled, her wrist twisting in Davis' tight grip. She cried out from the pain, which only seemed to make Davis wrench her along harder.

"Bring some chains from the stern," he ordered when they reached the hold. Old Ruddick lit another lantern, leaving the first perched on the lip of a low crate closest to the ladder. He limped off toward the holding pens of the animals. The foul smells of cow dung, bilge waters and dankness swirled around her. She took small breaths and tried to imagine the fresh sea air on deck.

As Davis clamped manacles on her, Jennie suddenly realized how similar he was to Red Bull. She looked at him with disdain, her teeth grinding.

"We may not have chains for all of you heathen convicts, but we certainly have enough for the likes of you." His breath was sour as he breathed into her face.

She jerked her head away.

"Turn away from me now all you like," he goaded, breathing heavily. "You'll soon be begging me for favours." He smirked and slowly swiped his hand across her chest.

Not again! Jennie squirmed from his touch and he smiled more, his eyes lighting with pleasure. She suddenly let herself go slack like she'd done once with Red Bull. The gleam in his eyes turned to anger. He slapped her face.

Her right cheek stung. Her head rattled. She concentrated on the scraping and clanging of chains and Old Ruddick's uneven footsteps heading in their direction.

Within a few moments Old Ruddick reappeared, dragging thick chains in one hand and carrying the lantern in the other. Davis looped the chains around a stack of crates, roughly binding Jennie upright to them. The heavy metal links bit painfully against her waist and cut into her hips. When he'd finished and stepped back to assess his handiwork, Jennie looked at him with loathing.

He stared at her with an air of superiority and snorted. "No food or water for forty-eight hours," he ordered Old Ruddick. "Leave no lantern lit."

The old sailor gave a nod of compliance, but kept his head averted, stepping aside when Davis strode toward the ladder.

"I didn't steal the coins," she shouted after him in a last effort of appeal. She didn't want to be left alone in the dark. "You have to find the real thief."

He ignored her, stomped up the ladder and slammed the hatch lid down. The sudden draft of air extinguished the first lantern and she was left in the semi-darkness. She sagged against her shackles, too weary to fight anymore.

She'd forgotten Old Ruddick's presence until he cleared his throat next to her. She jerked her head around and took in his leathery face, now shadowed with compassion.

"I didn't steal the coins," she whimpered.

"I know you didn't, lass," he said, looking steadily at her.

"I don't know why someone..." Jennie stopped. Had she just heard him right? She refocused. "What did you say?"

"I know you didn't, but I can't prove it, more's the pity." He looked at her steadily.

"But what do you know?" Jennie grasped at the thin shred of hope.

"Just that there is some conspiracy afoot. Beyond that I cannot discern."

"But even that is something. Can you tell it to Nate? Please," she pleaded.

He pursed his lips without commenting on her request.

"I have to go now. The dark won't be so bad, if you look toward the hatch. I'll not shut it tight. There'll be a tiny crack of light that may bring you comfort, lass."

Down the passageway, he extinguished the last lantern and eased his unsteady limbs up the ladder. As promised, he closed the hatch gently after he'd passed through.

The creaking of the ship was more eerie than ever. Jennie's breath came in short gasps as her fear of being left alone in the dark returned. It would be hours before the watch would change and sailors would switch places, coming back and forth to the hold, allowing in the light and some fresh air. There might be sailors sleeping somewhere down there with her, but she couldn't see or hear them. She could only hear the rustling of the livestock and the ship's creaking.

It seemed to take forever before her eyes adjusted. Old Ruddick was right though. Seeing the crack of light around the edge of the hatch lid did help. The stench below was overpowering, yet her stomach ached too. She'd only had the biscuit and some water the day before. She'd expected cooked oatmeal or something more substantial for breakfast, now that they had some food supplies. But that was no longer possible.

Suddenly she felt a nibble at her bare foot. She kicked it away. *Ugh!!* A rat! How had any of the women endured lying down here on the floor the night before?

Without being able to see or move, Jennie was stuck with no defences against more rats or bugs and other crawling, biting things. She swallowed hard and tried to imagine it was nighttime and that the crack of light from the hatch was the moon and the stars peeking out of the sky.

She closed her eyes and thought of home; her mother and sisters, safe and warm, sitting by their window in early evening watching the stars emerge. The first bright one that came out shortly after sunset – the evening star – was the one upon which each of them made their wishes.

Star light, star bright, first star I see tonight, I wish I may, I wish I might, have the wish, I wish tonight, played through her mind. Jennie wished hard to be back home again, forever free.

The minutes dragged, and the hours passed. She swooned from lack of food and water. She no longer had any saliva to brush her tongue over her lips. Her throat was closing up, her breathing was laboured. Then she knew no more.

CHAPTER NINETEEN

"SHE'S FAINTED. Get her some water."

Muffled voices reached Jennie's ears from somewhere far off. She sensed subdued light, a voice calling her, but she could not will herself to respond.

Sometime later a damp cloth patted her face and pressed against her cracked lips. She tried to rouse herself, but the stupor had her in its grip. It wasn't until she felt a trickle of water running awkwardly into the side of her mouth, held painfully open by a man's rough hand, that she became somewhat wakeful. Through blurry eyes she looked into Nate's worried face for a moment, but it wobbled and faded.

She heard Meadows' muted shout, "Fetch the keys from the captain!"

There were hurried footsteps up the ladder and someone's strong arms held her upright.

"We should have checked on her sooner," Nate chided.

"And not allowed Davis the upper hand," agreed Meadows.

A damp cloth swabbed at her face again.

Voices were clearer now, though she felt distant and disconnected. She opened her eyes. Closed them again. A rattling of keys, the loosening of chains, then she sagged against a man's warm body. Strong arms encircled her; she nestled in, unable to stand, unwilling to let go of safety and solace.

After a time, she looked up groggily to find Nate's concerned face above her again. She pulled away with an effort, realizing how close their bodies were. He pressed a cup to her lips and helped her drink.

Gradually, her senses returned. Her eyes skimmed Meadows hovering with Alice at his side.

"I was so worried about you," Alice said. She seemed unsure whether to go to Jennie or not.

"Thank you, Alice," Jennie murmured. Suddenly awash with gratitude, she held out her arms. Alice raced into them, clutching her tightly.

"Thank heavens Alice fretted so, or we'd have never known what state they'd left you in," said Nate, helping to keep her standing straight.

"It was Angus who helped me. He asked Old Ruddick," she whispered, half afraid she would get them into trouble.

Jennie noticed Angus standing by the ladder, clutching the captain's keys.

She smiled at him. "Thank you, Angus."

He nodded and clambered back through the hatch.

Jennie let her chin rest on the top of Alice's head, feeling the soft warmth of the young girl's trembling body. She allowed herself to collapse into Alice's embrace for some moments, much like she'd held her youngest sister, Anne, close the day the coppers had plucked her from her family and home. She was as afraid to let go of the warm affection as she had been that day.

She heard Meadows again. "Can the two of you manage to bring her on deck? I am going to have a harsh word or two with Captain MacGregor."

"Yes, sir," said Nate.

"Oh, yes," said Alice, looking at Jennie with a tear-streaked face.

Meadows headed off. With Nate on one side and Alice on the other, Jennie stumbled to the ladder. In the end Nate half-carried her up. Sarah was there to grab her as she emerged through the hatch.

"Oh, you poor lamb," said Sarah, as she helped Jennie settle onto a nest of blankets. "Angus, some food for her, if you please."

The cabin boy reached into his pocket and drew out a piece of hardtack. Brushing it off with his grubby hands, he handed it to Jennie.

She took it from him gratefully, and began gnawing at it. Her stomach was so empty it ached.

"I'll get something more," he said, and scampered off to the galley.

"We'll get you better than that filthy bit," said Sarah, reaching to take it away.

Jennie brushed her hand off gently. "I am so hungry, this tastes like a feast," she said.

Alice knelt beside her, holding a cup of water. Sarah clucked about, trying to make Jennie more comfortable.

"I can see you are in good hands," said Nate with a brief smile, before he disappeared.

She'd forgotten he was still there. Jennie watched his long confident strides. She now owed him for rescuing her several times over. She blushed to think that he'd held her in his arms just a short time ago and how much she'd liked the sensation.

Fanny and Hildy rushed to Jennie and began to examine her. Jennie groaned when Hildy touched her hip.

Fanny bent over to look at Jennie's face.

"Where's her leather pouch?" she asked. "We need a poultice for her swollen face."

"I have it hidden," said Alice, setting down the cup and dashing off.

"Which lout smacked you?" she asked. "You have a right

good bruise."

"Davis," Jennie whispered, sinking into the blankets. All the muscles in her body hurt at once.

"I'd like to get that evil brute back," fumed Fanny.

"You'd only end up treated like her," reminded Hildy.

"Yeah, but at least I'd have some satisfaction," Fanny retorted. She turned her attention back to Jennie. "Now how are we going to fix you up? Will a poultice help?"

"It'll have to do," Sarah said.

"Use the yarrow," Jennie mumbled. "There should be some salve."

"There isn't so awful much left," Alice apologized when she returned and opened the pouch. "Angus and I gathered up as much as we could after your pouch got dumped. Some of it got kind of muddled up, and some was wasted."

"That's all right, dearie," said Sarah, patting her cheek. "There's enough here for now. Saves us from mixing it."

"Good," murmured Jennie.

She closed her eyes and let the women fuss over her. The coolness of the poultice soothed her face. As they spread the cream mixture on her other bruises, she relaxed.

"I've brought you some broth," said Angus some minutes later. "Cook says that's best for a body who hasn't had anything much to eat in a while."

"Cook's a smart man," said Sarah, taking it from him. "And a kind one. Please tell him thank you."

"I will," said Angus.

"I'm grateful for all that you've done for me too," Jennie added.

Angus looked pleased as he sauntered off.

Accepting a spoonful of broth from Fanny, Jennie felt the soothing hot liquid dribble down her throat all the way to her stomach. After a few more satisfying spoonfuls, Jennie took the bowl and sipped quickly from the edge.

"Not too fast," warned Sarah.

Jennie drained the last drop and lay back down on the blankets. Alice and the women tucked her in and sat beside her, chatting.

From a little farther down the deck raised voices caught Jennie's attention. She lifted her head and saw Captain MacGregor berating Davis for his treatment of Jennie. Meadows and Nate stood beside the captain, glaring at the angry-faced sailor. Red Bull stood a few steps to the side of Davis, his jaw clenched.

"But she's a thief!" he protested.

"You certainly had no right to treat her so poorly," the captain berated him.

"Besides, she didn't steal the coins," Nate challenged.

"You saw the evidence yourself," Davis snarled back. "We found the coins in her possession."

"You found them in a leather pouch she'd been using," corrected Meadows. "Anyone could have put them there. Even you!"

"And I charge that someone else did," Nate said.

"As well, not all of the gold coins were retrieved," Captain MacGregor interrupted. "Do you have any ideas about that?"

Davis flicked a glance at Red Bull, almost too quick to be discernible, but Jennie saw it. And so did Nate.

Nate whirled around and confronted Red Bull.

"What do you know about the missing coins?" Nate pressed.

Red Bull took a step back. "Why would I know anything?"

"I saw him pick up a coin," Jennie called out in a weak voice. She tried to rise, and although the women around her tried to hold her back, she persisted. "This is about me. I need to go."

They helped Jennie up and she hobbled over to the group of men.

"I saw him stuff one of the coins into his shirt yesterday," she said, staring down Red Bull. "And I'm sure he must have taken others."

Nate and Meadows advanced on Red Bull. He continued backing up until he was against the bulwark.

"It's not right that you take the word of a common thief over me."

"I want this man searched." Meadows ordered. "Coombs, Edwards, hold him. Nate you do the honours."

Surprisingly, Red Bull relaxed a little. Coombs and Edwards pinned his arms as Nate searched his clothing and patted him down. Captain MacGregor observed, sombre-faced.

Jennie watched in growing amazement as Red Bull succumbed to a thorough search with a faint hint of a smirk. Davis looked alarmed. Jennie scrutinized him closer. Was he in on it too?

Nate splayed his hands in exasperation when he couldn't find anything. With a thoughtful expression, Meadows ordered Coombs and Edwards to release him.

Jennie was disappointed, but then reasoned Red Bull was probably smart enough not to hide the coins on his person. Maybe he'd given them to Davis. She made a small clearing noise in her throat loud enough to attract Meadows' attention and pointedly glanced at Davis.

Meadows eyed her and then Davis. "Captain, may I have your permission to search Davis?"

"Aye," Captain MacGregor assented.

"I protest," Davis sputtered, but to no avail.

"These two are in on this together, I warrant." MacGregor stared sullenly at Davis.

"I know nothing about any missing coins," Davis asserted. He rigidly yielded to being pinned by Coombs and Edwards, continuing to object indignantly as his pockets were searched and his body patted.

"Nothing." Nate stared hard at Davis, who righted his clothes when they were done.

Angus and Old Ruddick had crept closer throughout the interactions.

"I reckon they hid them coins somewhere on board," Old Ruddick mentioned.

Jennie scanned the deck. Her eyes alighted on the jolly boat. Red Bull and Davis had spent an inordinate amount of time by it.

Nate and Meadows followed the direction of her eyes.

"Perhaps we need to search on the deck," said Meadows, striding toward the stern.

The others followed, including Red Bull, breathing heavily.

Meadows and Nate flipped the boat over and began probing under the gunwale.

"What might this be?" Nate drew out a tightly tied cloth on a lengthy cord. He fumbled the bundle open.

"Aha! Captain MacGregor, it looks like we found the rest of your coins." Nate held out his hand where the gold winked in the sun.

"And extra to boot," added Meadows, counting them. "There seem to be more than you reported missing. Now, I wonder where they came from."

Red Bull's mouth gaped open, but no words came out for a moment.

"I've never seen them before!" he sputtered. He furled his brows, feigning innocence.

Davis shrugged his shoulders. "First time I seen it."

"I'd say it came from a certain piece of wreckage on the water," suggested Nate, flashing a smile Jennie's way. "This cloth looks familiar." He held up the bag, showing the insignia of the *Emily Anne*.

A surge of relief rose through Jennie's body.

Red Bull blustered, "Coombs could have put it there."

Coombs stared hard at Red Bull. He began swearing and defending his innocence.

Meadows shook his head. "We know you were the only one who could have done it."

Captain MacGregor eyed Red Bull with outrage.

Red Bull's eyes darted in fear like those of a cornered animal looking for a way of escape.

"Arrest this man." Captain MacGregor signalled to two sailors. Coombs quickly volunteered too.

Red Bull struggled, but they were quick to restrain him.

"I think you might have needed some help in procuring my coins," MacGregor said, "and I'd warrant the girl was not the one to give it to you." He gave Jennie a brief smile, then turned back to Red Bull. "You certainly had to have inside information."

MacGregor turned to Davis with a grim expression. "Lieutenant Davis, I charge you with theft." He waved over Old Ruddick and another of his sailors.

Davis started to protest. "It must have been Angus! He had access to your quarters. I had nothing to do..."

"Blaming a young boy! What nerve!" Fanny shook her fist at Davis.

"Indeed!" said Sarah.

Jennie smiled at the passion of the two women.

"Save your breath, Lieutenant," said Nate. "We already know you were involved."

"How?" Davis staggered back, as Old Ruddick and the other sailor grabbed his arms.

"Let's just say a wise old owl and a couple of young birdies told us," said Nate.

"Chain them to the mainmast, until we decide what to do with them," ordered the captain with a quick glance at Meadows.

Meadows nodded.

Coombs and two sailors led Red Bull away. Davis and his guards followed.

Jennie rushed forward to thank Meadows and Nate. "And

thank you too, Captain MacGregor," she said.

"I didn't want to believe a nice lass like you would have stolen from me, though I couldn't see around the facts," he admitted.

"Just who were the two little birdies and wise owl?" asked Jennie.

Meadows chuckled. Captain MacGregor's eyes twinkled. Nate tilted his head toward Alice.

"Alice, and...," Jennie paused, "Angus!" She grinned at the cabin boy, who beamed beside a blushing Alice.

Jennie's thoughts turned to who might be the wise old owl. *Old? Of course!*

"Old Ruddick!" she cried, suddenly remembering he'd told her he believed she was innocent, but couldn't prove it.

She looked over to the where the wiry man uncoiled ropes to use on the prisoners. He dipped his head and gave her a toothy grin.

"But what did they know?" Jennie turned back to the captain.

"It wasn't so much what each knew individually, but what we were able to piece together. Especially with what you told us."

"Each heard a little of the pair's plans to steal the coins and get rid of you," said Nate. "But thanks to you, we were already suspicious."

Jennie kept her eyes on Nate as he talked. Her vision began to swim. Suddenly she felt weak. Perhaps she was sicker than she knew. She wobbled.

Sarah caught her under the arms just before she tumbled over.

"Time to get you something more to eat and then abed," said Sarah.

"I'll take her." Nate picked up Jennie and cradled her in his arms. She laid her head against Nate's broad chest, comforted by his strong hold. He wasn't even breathing hard when he set her down in her nest of blankets. In fact, he didn't seem to be breathing at all.

"Bloody hell!" Old Ruddick's curse came from across the deck.

Jennie peered past Nate where Ruddick was picking himself up after being knocked down by Davis, who was attempting to escape a sailor's hold. The sailor hung on, as Davis dragged and chopped at the sailor's arms with the edge of his hands. The sailor finally had to let go. Once freed, Davis sprinted toward the jolly boat.

With the distraction, Red Bull bellowed. He butted his head into Coombs, then swung a punch at the neck of one of the sailors. The sailor's eyes rolled back in his head, and he collapsed. Coombs kept a grip on Red Bull's shirt. Red Bull kicked him between his legs. Coombs crumpled. Red Bull sprang over to Davis, and the two men pushed the jolly boat over the side of the ship.

Nate, Meadows and other sailors bounded toward them as the two prisoners lowered the boat, the ropes slipping easily over the side. The jolly boat hit the water with a hard slap. Nate grabbed at Red Bull and Meadows reached for Davis, but the pair eluded them.

Captain MacGregor strode across the deck, shouting orders for the crew to lower the sails and heave to. Coombs, Old Ruddick and the other sailors recovered enough to pursue their quarry. Jennie was up on her knees, the other women watching the fracas incredulously beside her.

Red Bull dodged his pursuers and faked a move around a pile of sails. He headed back around to the bulwark where the jolly boat had gone down, Ruddick in pursuit.

Red Bull managed to fling a leg over the side. Nate grabbed his other leg. They struggled, Nate trying to pull Red Bull back onto the ship.

Nearby, Davis fought off Meadows and other sailors. In a moment of freedom, Davis made a run for it and dived over the side. A moment later, they heard a resounding splash. Angus peered overboard. Yelps and weak splashing noises continued for a few more moments, then nothing.

"Didn't make it," Angus reported back to the women, shock on his face. "I guess he couldn't swim."

Jennie turned her attention back to Red Bull. He tried to stay balanced on the railing, one leg either side, while he pummelled Nate about his face and neck. Meadows hastened over. Red Bull flailed again and managed to break free of Nate. Just as Meadows reached for him, Red Bull lost his balance. He plunged overboard, screamed once, then for a short moment there was silence.

Splack!!

Jennie clung to Sarah's hand. Angus turned to them, his mouth gaping. Nate bowed his head against the railing. Meadows stood stunned beside him. At last Angus announced, "Hit the jolly boat." He swallowed hard, then turned to vomit over the side.

Captain MacGregor sucked in a breath. "Well, then, I guess I'm in need of a new first mate for our return trip." He turned to Meadows. "It's yours. If you want it. We'll talk later." He marched off to his quarters.

Jennie buried her face in her hands, sobbing. She felt a strange mixture of exhaustion and an enormous sense of relief. No more Red Bull, no more accusations of her stealing gold coins. No more...what? What was next on the horizon for her?

CHAPTER TWENTY

JENNIE WOKE ON THE DECK with a strange squeaking in her ears. She blinked and looked around. The door of the captain's quarters was firmly shut. She couldn't see anything else on deck that would make that particular shrill noise.

Dawn had just broken and the ship rocked gently, the sails snapping occasionally. Old Ruddick was at the wheel and several other sailors were on watch, some perched on the rigging and one in the crow's nest. They were peering at something starboard in the water. The high-pitched squeaky sounds continued.

Extracting herself carefully from between Alice and Sarah, Jennie pulled a blanket over her shoulders. Clutching it to her chest, she eased to the railing and leaned over. Several huge grey-blue fish dived in and out of the water in fluid, graceful motions. As they swam beside the ship, they chattered in high-pitched sounds. Jennie laughed as some even stood on their tails and jiggered across the surface, showing off for her.

"Good to see you're up and about," said Nate, sliding in quietly beside her.

She hadn't sensed his approach, but his sudden presence and gentle manner somehow fit with the tranquillity of the pale pink hues of the morning and the peaceful smooth creatures swimming below. A feeling of serenity and hope filled her heart. For a moment, she wondered if she was in a pleasant dream where her life was her own again. She glanced at Nate to make sure he was real.

"A pod of dolphins," he said in a low voice.

"I've never seen dolphins before," she responded softly, not wanting to break the spell. "Dolphins." She said the word again, enjoying the way it sounded.

"Probably means we're close to land," Nate added.

"To Tenerife?" Jennie asked.

"Or nearby islands."

"That means we'll be leaving this ship soon," Jennie surmised.

"Yes, and the captain will have to decide what to do with us."

Jennie peeked at Nate. What did he mean by *us?*

"Meadows is probably going to stay on with the *Lady Margaret*, at least until it finishes its voyage and returns home," Nate said. "He'd prefer to be back with a British-crewed ship."

"And Coombs and Edwards?" she asked.

"They will probably stay on too, if asked. A captain can always use more bodies. He's lost a couple of men, besides Davis and the doctor, along the way."

"And you?" Jennie asked lightly.

"I don't know where I fit," said Nate. "I'm no sailor, that's for sure."

"You seem to do well on a ship."

Nate chuckled softly. "Not at all."

"But you know so much about the ocean, and you rescued us and then saved Kate," Jennie responded.

"That was with a rowboat," he said with a grin. "I wouldn't know which sail to hoist to save my life."

"But you risked *your* life and saved so many of *our* lives. You collected us together, got us organized and tied the platform together."

"I'm *resourceful*, as my father would say. That's all. We lived on a river and had a rowboat for fishing, which we had to do a lot for food, but I'm not fond of being on the open water."

Jennie looked at him in surprise. "Then why were you working on a ship as a guard?"

"I wanted to see a new land, have an adventure," he said, shrugging. "Besides, there were too many mouths to feed at home and we needed the money. I thought I might even find work in Van Diemen's Land and send money home." He grimaced. "I had no idea what it would be like."

"To be on a ship, you mean? Or a guard for convicts?" Jennie asked carefully.

"Both."

She waited for him to say more. He stared pensively out at the dolphins. They were chattering and swimming away into the horizon, now streaked with beams of bright sunlight.

"And so?" she finally prompted.

"I don't like either."

Jennie turned to him, leaning her back against the bulwark. "Why?"

He looked down at his hands. "The heartlessness of it all. The sailors are a rough lot; their masters can be cruel and the life is hard and unforgiving. The men have nothing much else in their lives." He raised his head and stared out at the rippling ocean.

"You don't think they were, like you, taking a job to feed their families?"

"Some may have started that way, I guess, escaping from something else," said Nate. "But most are just trying to survive from day to day any way they can because they've got nothing to go back to."

"And being a guard?" Jennie asked more boldly.

"There weren't many choices, and my father pressed me into it. But most guards are brutal. They love to bully and hold sway over others, especially when it comes to women. They're even worse than the sailors!" His eyes flashed with contempt. "Many are more criminal than those they hold captive...like Chilcott – Red Bull was."

She gave him a puzzled look. "So you know about Red Bull's past?"

He nodded. "Yes. He bragged about it one night when he was drunk, after he'd beaten Lizzie. About how he'd murdered another man and had gotten away with it because they didn't have enough evidence to convict him." Nate went on to tell her how someone had thwarted Red Bull who had planned the murder to look like an accident...on some lake in the North Country. But those who were involved in the investigation knew the bruises and cuts on the victim were from more than hitting a head on the side of a boat, or being washed about in the rocks on shore.

"And Lizzie recognized him from the Old Bailey where he was tried," Jennie said thoughtfully, almost to herself. Her mind flitted regretfully over the memory of Lizzie. If only she hadn't tried to bribe Red Bull.

Nate nodded again. "Recognition by happenstance. Only then, she used an assumed name. She was working as a..." Nate stopped, blushing.

"A doxy," Jennie filled in for him matter-of-factly. She smiled over at Fanny, emerging through the hatch. Jennie no longer had any qualms about what doxies were, or what they did, or about speaking of them openly. Lizzie and Fanny had become her friends. They'd only been doing what was necessary to survive.

Nate looked at her with discomfiture.

"You learn things you'd rather not, being in such close confines with convicts," she said with the hint of a smile still on her lips. "Mostly you learn to stick up for yourself and what you believe in."

"You do the best that you can do," said Nate.

"Though, look where it gets you sometimes," said Jennie with a hint of bitter regret.

"You, too, were only trying to survive," said Nate tenderly. "I'd probably have done the same."

Her eyes watered, but she held her emotions in check.

"And what about you? How do you feel?" she almost whispered.

"I despise what's happening in England. The poverty, the hunger and the despair. Most of these women – including you – wouldn't be here, except that you were hungry, or had families that were hungry."

"At least *you* found honest work," Jennie said, feeling her face flush. She glanced away and then back again, swallowing. "I should have tried harder. I still shouldn't have stolen."

"You *did* have honest work. Your landlord stole what was owed to you and your family. He had no call for the way he treated you in your work, or over what his wife tossed in the rubbish, which was clearly spoilt. He should be here, not you!" He clasped her hand. "There wasn't any other decent work for you to do."

Jennie was shocked that Nate knew so much about her. She was sure she hadn't told him. She glanced over at Alice and Sarah, who were busy feeding Mary. They would never say anything. Meadows must have told him.

Nate continued gravely, "I couldn't find any other work besides this quickly enough to help my family. Nor do I have any other training, and I abhor what I do!"

He clenched the railing. "This work wouldn't be necessary, if people had some way to feed themselves. The government is to blame for that, and for locking decent people up because they're starving. I want to do something more worthwhile in life. Something with honour. I'd rather starve than do this again."

"Brave words coming from a naive young pup," Captain MacGregor interrupted.

Jennie tensed. She hadn't heard the captain's approach. Nate dropped her hand and faced him.

"Only speaking the truth," he said humbly.

"Aye, the truth, as you know it. And you may be right at that." Captain MacGregor looked at them thoughtfully. "After what I've just heard, I guess it's out of the question to ask you if you'd like to continue on with my ship. It would be good to have a hard-working young man of your morals amongst us."

Jennie was proud of the captain's regard for Nate. Nate was the nicest man she knew and she wished she wouldn't have to be parted from him when they docked. She knew that was exactly what would happen though. She was still a convict and he a guard.

Nate shook his head. "Sorry, sir. But I thank you for your offer."

"What will you do then?" Captain MacGregor asked.

"I have no idea at the moment." He shrugged again. "I guess that partly depends on you and what you and Meadows decide about the rest of us, once we land at Tenerife." Nate stared into the captain's eyes.

Jennie's heart did a little flutter at the "us" again.

"About that," said the captain, breaking the glance and stroking his chin. "Seeing as how you want to change your post, we can probably find a ship to get you back to England and your family."

"Begging your pardon, sir," Nate said in a hoarse voice, "but that would be the last place I'd like to return to. There is nothing for me there, except more poverty and hunger."

Captain MacGregor tilted his head in thought. "The Commonwealth has many countries in its realm with opportunities, but none more full of prospects right now than the new Province of Canada."

Nate's eyes lit up. "That sounds like a good choice."

Jennie's mind became alert. She'd heard about immigration there. A cousin of her mother's had gone to the Province of Canada a year earlier and had reported success.

"There's a good likelihood that there will be ships in Tenerife heading that way," the captain said.

"We'll see, I guess," said Nate. There was slight glimmer of hope in his accompanying smile. "Thank you, sir." He gave the captain a little bow.

When he straightened again, his expression had turned serious. "That is a fine idea for me, but, by us I meant the women too."

He moved closer to Jennie and indicated the women grouped in the centre of the ship. Jennie clutched the blanket tighter around her.

Nate's close presence gave Jennie added courage to ask loudly, so the others nearby could hear. "Yes, what about us, sir? Us...uh...convicts?"

Nate touched her elbow in encouragement.

Captain MacGregor said, "You'll probably be put onto a ship bound for England to start for the Van Diemen's Land colony again. Unless there's one headed there that has space when we arrive in Tenerife. Then they could decide to send you straight there."

Jennie gulped. "Is there something else you might consider, sir?"

Behind her, she heard the women murmuring, but not loud enough to discern what they were saying. They were all apprehensive about their futures.

The captain waved a hand as if to dismiss her. "I don't hold with most of the laws, but what you want is out of the question. I have my reputation and my appointment to take into account." He stomped away.

"What will we do now?" Jennie headed over to the other women to relay her exchange with the captain. She threw the blanket down in frustration.

"There must be a way we can convince him," said Fanny.

"Maybe we could offer to make ourselves useful," Sarah said. She looked over the ship. "This tub could use a good cleaning."

"That might be the way to get into his good graces," Hildy said, "but that's not going to convince him to free us."

"Too bad he has to tell anyone about us at all," said Alice, frowning.

"That's it!" Jennie grabbed Alice and swung her around. "I'll see if I can convince him."

As Jennie hurried off, she heard the women discussing what to clean first.

"Angus, fetch us a bucket and a mop," Sarah called out.

"I'll coil these ropes out of the way," said Fanny.

Hildy volunteered to sort out the sails that needed fixing from the pile at the stern.

Jennie approached the captain hopefully, standing beside him for a few moments as he stared out to sea. She noted an occasional bird on the wing in the distance. They must only be a couple of days from Tenerife.

At last Jennie broke the silence. "Sir, I *may* have a solution about us. That is, it would depend on you...if you'd be willing."

Captain MacGregor motioned for her to proceed.

Jennie bit her bottom lip. "Seeing as how there were very few survivors from the shipwreck, maybe the authorities need not know about the rest of us at all."

She clasped her hands in front of her waist and continued, "Maybe you tell them we all perished. You could forget you ever rescued any of us, and just let us go our own way."

Jennie paused to judge the captain's reaction, glancing at the women nodding their encouragement. Nate sauntered over to her and the captain.

"Not turn you over to the authorities?" Captain MacGregor said with a frown. "That's out of the question."

Nate cut in. "The authorities probably won't want to concern themselves with the fate of a few poor women they don't know what to do with anyway. They'll be more set on compensation for the loss of the ship than the *cargo*, once they discover it was lost in a storm."

The captain rubbed his chin as he thought.

Nate continued, "They'd likely prefer to wash their hands of the women entirely. Maybe you would too, sir, especially if you're not keen on preparing the heap of official documents required."

As the captain considered the situation, Jennie asked quietly, "*Would* you consider letting us go?" She took a deep breath. "I doubt anyone would find out, especially now that Red Bull – I mean, Chilcott – is gone."

Nate said, "Coombs and Edwards will be happy they have work on your ship, and I'm sure I can convince them and Meadows to say all convicts were *lost* at sea, as it were."

"Please, sir." Jennie couldn't keep the pleading from her voice.

She glanced at Sarah and Alice again, holding their hands up to their chests with bowed heads as they waited for the captain's answer. The others had stopped working and looked on wide-eyed.

"Still there are those who *might* speak," said the captain hesitantly.

Jennie motioned Sarah and Alice to join her. "None of us would say anything," Jennie added hopefully. "I'm sure the other women would agree to a vow of silence without a second thought."

"Indeed we would," said Sarah.

"Yes, sir," Alice agreed.

Jennie continued, as the other women made their way over. "We'll make our own way, just disappear, and you'll never hear from us again. I promise."

The women nodded.

The captain wiped a drip of spittle off the corner of his mouth with his sleeve. He was a drinker and probably wouldn't be able to hold his own counsel.

Jennie added, "If any rumours surface, you can always say we tricked you, that we told you we were ordinary passengers."

The captain frowned. "I *might* be convinced to hold my tongue with the right persuasion."

Jennie's hopes plummeted. Surely he knew that the women had no money to pay a bribe and nothing else with which to trade. Another thought made her blanch. She certainly wasn't going to become a doxy on this ship, if that's what he was suggesting.

Then she thought again about being on a convict ship and the beatings. Would they end up on another ship with a captain who sanctioned cruel treatment? Maybe being a doxy would be an alternative she would have to consider seriously. But she certainly wasn't desperate enough to do so yet.

The captain spoke casually, "Of course, it was *my* goodwill that rescued you and brought you all on board *my* ship without any thought of recompense." He eyed them expectantly.

Jennie stared at him coldly. She had not thought him to be so unscrupulous, even if he was a man often in his cups.

"Wait a moment, Captain MacGregor," Sarah said, stepping forward. "Most of us are able-bodied women, or at least we will be if you feed us. We could cook, clean the ship and mend sails."

She pointed to the women already hard at work. "And Jennie could tend to your sick."

The captain snorted.

"But aren't any of those things worth anything to you?" asked Jennie.

The captain threw her a look of disdain.

"Won't it at least help pay for our passage?" Sarah asked.

"Not enough." Captain MacGregor narrowed his eyes slightly as he scanned the sea.

Now what? Jennie knew he was considering the sailors on his ship and how far he could trust them. She learned from Old Ruddick that several men had been in cahoots with Davis in selling off the ship's supplies before they even set sail. They had hoped to overpower the captain and the ship mid-voyage and prey upon any unsuspecting ships that happened by. Or at the very least, sell off some of the illegal contraband that they'd smuggled on board in place of provisions. They'd want a hefty fee for keeping the women's secret.

Nate raised his eyebrows. "Did we not bring you extra food and goods salvaged from the wreckage? That should help somewhat."

"Indeed, it does," the captain assured him quickly.

Jennie regarded him with a touch of disapproval. "And I believe the real thieves on your ship were apprehended, thanks to Nate and Meadows. And your coins were returned to you intact."

"Aye, this was appreciated too." Captain MacGregor clasped his hands in thanks, making a little bow toward them.

"And I recall that you procured extra gold coins, as well, from the ones Chilcott stole from the *Emily Anne*," Nate reminded him.

Jennie glared at Captain MacGregor. How dare he try to exploit them! She heaved a breath of disgust. She had thought he was a decent sort of man. But now she wanted to kick him in the shins. Nate held her elbow, sensing her increasing anger.

"Aye, that is also true," said the captain, rubbing at his beard. "You understand that's all well and good for the ship and the morale of the men, well, and for *me*. As you pointed out, I have had some compensation, so *I* might be convinced to keep my peace, but my crew...there's not nearly enough for me to share with them. Maybe they'd yammer to someone from another ship that you had been in Tenerife. They might be wanting something substantial for withholding certain information..." His words dwindled off.

"We have nothing else to offer," said Jennie flatly.

The captain deliberated for a few moments, then seemed to reach a decision. "No matter whatever you have to offer, I have my own skin to consider. There is no guarantee someone will not talk. I cannot risk my commission. Being captain of this ship, or maybe another, is my whole life. If I let you go, and it ever got out, I would be ruined. I'm sorry, but I can't help."

Jennie's spirits sank even more. Now what were they to do?

CHAPTER TWENTY-ONE

JENNIE STARED at the captain's retreating back. The other women dispersed, muttering in disappointment. They might have to wait months on Tenerife for a decision about their fate. Assuming a ship that would give them passage came their way, they might be taken home, jailed and transported again to Van Diemen's Land, or sent straight to the penal colony. No choice at all.

What would Tenerife be like? Where would they be held? Jennie's mind clashed with jumbled thoughts. Maybe they could escape, if they planned it right. They'd have to think of every possibility. She turned thoughtfully toward Sarah and the other women. Now was the time to enlist their help.

Jennie gathered Sarah, Alice, Kate, and Fanny to her and voiced her thoughts about escaping. "Do you think just we few should try to get away? With so many of us, I'm not sure we can all go," said Jennie, looking at the dozen women nearby.

"I say we all stick together," said Sarah. The others nodded. "They might be able to help us come up with a plan."

Fanny shrugged. "Why not? Even if they don't join us, they're not likely to squeal our plans to anyone given the risks to themselves."

Jennie motioned the other women over. They stood in a huddle amidship, their voices kept low while Jennie conveyed their intentions. She didn't need to do any convincing. They all wanted to be included.

"We have to think about how to get away, where we go, and how to get there," said Jennie.

Sarah added, "I think we'd all have to agree on the same destination to make it the easiest and safest."

She looked around the group and they all nodded.

"Yes, let's make sure we all get out together," said Hildy.

Jennie thought of the consequences if one of them was caught and tortured to talk. They'd have to make sure that didn't happen.

Fanny, ever the individual spirit, said, "We can make our separate ways after we get out of the captain's clutches and away from the law."

"Let's think about getting to safety first," said Sarah. "Where should we go?"

"What about the Province of Canada?" suggested Jennie. She recalled the excitement she'd felt when Captain MacGregor had suggested this for Nate.

"What would we do there?" asked Mary.

"With a new settlement like that, I'm sure there are lots of opportunities," said Hildy. "Probably better than anywhere else."

They mulled this over for a while, tossing out pros and cons. Jennie didn't know what she'd do either, but she was willing to take her chances. At least in the Province of Canada they hadn't accepted convicts like the Americans had done in the past. Maybe the people there wouldn't have jurisdiction, or be as prone to lock them up and send them back.

"Does anyone see any other viable option?" Jennie asked.

No one spoke.

"Then I suggest that's where we head," Sarah said.

"Is everyone in agreement?" asked Jennie. She eyed each individual until they responded. There was no hesitation.

"All right then, the Province of Canada's our destination."

"We'll have to make sure the story gets out that our ship sank and we were all lost. Otherwise, the law might come looking for us," said Kate.

A sudden wave of sadness clasped Jennie's stomach. Would her family hear about the shipwreck? Somehow she'd have to let them know she was still alive. At that moment, she vowed whatever choices came her way, some day she would see her mum and sisters again.

Jennie rallied. "Okay, now, what's our plan to get there?" She waited for ideas to surface.

"Maybe we could find a cargo or passenger ship to give us free passage, if we all offer to help on board," Mary suggested.

"Possible, but not practical. There are too many of us," objected Hildy.

"Maybe we will have to split up," said Fanny.

"Some of us wouldn't make it on our own," said Mary.

"Let's see what other options we can come up with first," said Jennie. "We have to think about where to stay hidden while we await passage."

"What about the convents?" Iris asked. "There are plenty on Tenerife, no matter where we land. We could hide in one or two for a while."

Fanny guffawed. "Yeah, the likes of us could dress in habits and walk around in plain sight."

"That's not such a bad idea," said Sarah.

"I was joking," Fanny said. Then she sobered. "You know, it might just work."

"But what about me?" asked Alice. "I couldn't be a nun at my age."

Sarah responded, "No, dearie, but you could pass as a child

in one of their orphanages."

"It would just be until we could find our passage to the new country," said Mary. "Pretending to be nuns might even help us get free passage."

"I like it," said Hildy.

Iris snipped, "It will be good to be in a house of God again and away from you heathen lot."

Everyone ignored her.

"All in favour of hiding in a convent?" Mary asked.

Everyone raised their hands. Excited whispers rustled through the huddle of women. They silenced suddenly when Nate approached them.

"Come with me," he said to Jennie and nodded to the others.

He led Jennie starboard. Sarah and Alice aided Kate. The others followed, assisting those who needed help.

"We'll be docking in a few hours." Ned pointed out to sea.

"What do you mean?" she asked.

His eyes followed a flock of gulls in the distance.

She recalled birds only flew close to land.

"Now look a little to your left," he directed.

Far on the horizon, fishing boats bobbed on the glistening water.

"We're near Tenerife!" Jennie caught her breath. Her future lay before her. But what would it bring? A life of servitude on a penal colony, or chancing the unknown in the Province of Canada? The women around her stared transfixed but subdued, probably wondering the same thing.

Puzzled, Nate looked at her. "I thought you would be happy to see land again."

"Not if it means I'll be imprisoned."

Jennie felt Nate's eyes on her as she walked away with a sad heart. The other women followed.

"We've got to finish making our plans quickly," she said

when they were out of earshot of the sailors.

She noticed Nate and Meadows had waylaid the captain in what seemed an animated conversation.

"How will we escape from Captain McGregor and his crew?" Jennie felt her temperature rise. There wasn't much time to plan. "Remember we're all in this together."

Sarah spoke first. "We have no money, doing chores for them obviously won't get us paid, and even if we were willing to trade our bodies, which we're *not*, there would be no guarantee they wouldn't renege on any deal we struck."

"And for sure we could never overpower the captain and the crew," said Hildy. "And sneaking off without being noticed is impossible."

"We need something else to bargain with," said Fanny.

"We may be able to negotiate something." Nate's voice behind them made them all jump.

Nate nodded and Meadows brought the captain over to them.

"Captain McGregor," Meadows prodded, "tell the women how you are willing to reconsider your decision to release them. I want them to hear, so there can be no misunderstandings."

The captain loosened the top button of his shirt and cleared his throat. "When we get to Tenerife, I would consider...looking the other way if a certain party of women were to disembark without aid and disappear."

The women grew excited, but Jennie scrutinized the captain.

"You'd be willing to do this? There wouldn't be any trickery?"

Captain MacGregor nodded. "Yes, I would, though I think a little recompense wouldn't be amiss."

"And I think, Captain MacGregor, you should reconsider your request in light of your situation," said Meadows.

The captain hesitated, weighing his chances of other compensation.

Meadows lost his patience. "I'm not without the ear of General Tottington, whom I'm sure will be none too pleased to hear of your drunken command of this vessel and the ineptness of your handling of the men, who have stolen merchandise from the company you work for, which, incidentally, belongs to *him*."

"Well, I, well..." MacGregor spluttered, his face turning purple. "If you put it that way, I shall withdraw my suggestion."

He bowed his head, but Jennie had seen how his eyes glowered at Meadows.

Jennie, too, had misgivings about the captain and his men. "What if someone from the *Lady Margaret* slips?" she whispered to Nate.

He gave her a slow smile. "He can always say he put everyone on another ship and washed his hands of us, and that he knows nothing more."

Jennie's attention was caught by Captain MacGregor asking the very thing she wanted to know next.

"Just how am I supposed to ensure that my men, once they are on shore or leave my employ, won't let their tongues wag?"

Meadows responded ruefully, "It would be in your best interest and theirs, Captain MacGregor, to warn the crew that they could all be turned in for grand larceny and plans of mutiny. I'm fairly certain if you do, the threat of prosecution will hold their counsel too."

The captain nodded, his face sullen and wary.

"If that's not enough, when we've docked, we'll arrange for the women to leave the ship under cover of darkness, while most of your crew is asleep. Old Ruddick will keep his counsel, so leave him on watch. Angus too, if you have a mind for it. Then none of you will know details of how or where they went."

The captain tilted his head in taciturn agreement. "Aye, and I have your word for it that naught will be said about my command?"

"As long as you keep up your end of the bargain," said Meadows. "I will be with you until we return to Britain to see that you do. I also have acquaintances who will keep me informed afterwards."

Captain MacGregor pressed his lips together and contemplated Meadows. Then he reached out a hand. Meadows shook it. The captain stalked off toward his cabin.

Jennie sucked in a deep breath. "The captain is really willing to let us go?" she asked in amazement.

Meadows nodded.

Jennie persisted, "And you're willing to do so too?"

Meadows shrugged. "You've been through so much, I think you've paid for your crimes."

"We're really going to be freed?" asked Alice.

Meadows nodded again.

"Oh, thank you so very much," Jennie grabbed Meadows' hand and shook it so hard his arm jiggled.

Meadows smiled and released her grip. The other women gathered around, cheering Meadows and Nate. Amid everyone's tears and hugs and pats on the backs, Jennie was overwhelmed with emotion. She managed to drag herself away to thank Meadows again. Though they weren't out of danger yet, a beacon of hope shone brightly through for the future.

"How can I – we – ever thank you? This will make such a difference to our lives."

"You might not be wanting to thank me yet," said Meadows. "What will become of you after Tenerife is an even greater problem."

"Yes. I have no idea what I'll do." Jennie shifted away and studied the sea. Her chest tensed when Meadows stole a glance at her.

"If you don't mind me saying so, you'd make a right good doctor's aide."

Pleasure shot through Jennie, but she knew this was unrealistic to hope for. "No one would want me. I'd never be able to get the training I need."

"With the needle skills you already have and your successes with healing," he nodded toward Kate, "I daresay you could learn as an apprentice with any doctor worth his salt."

She regarded Meadows thoughtfully. "I have no idea where or how that could ever be possible."

Meadows said, "For sure you would not be welcome in England, lest they discover you've not completed your sentence."

She calmed herself and thought about the possibilities. If news of them perishing in the shipwreck was to be leaked, she would disappear from the records. She could return to England on a different ship and pretend to be someone else. But living a lie was not what she wanted. She'd still be no closer to her family, and couldn't put them in harm's way for harbouring her.

"England would not be the destination I'd choose," she said. "I'd never really be free there."

She glanced sideways at Meadows. He shrugged. "Where you go is for you to decide. Just keep in mind that the fewer who know, the better, including me." He patted her shoulder and walked away.

Nate joined her side. "Where you'll go and what you'll do once you get off the ship is a bit of problem."

Jennie led Nate back around to talk to the other women, "We already have a few plans of our own. If they're in agreement, we'll tell you."

"You tell him," said Sarah. "The rest of us will keep away any busybodies that might overhear."

The women scattered.

"Brilliant idea," said Nate after Jennie filled him in on their plan to hide in convents until they could leave the island. "Though, there's the little detail of finding convents to take all of you. I'll see what I can do to help."

"You will?"

'Indeed." Then Nat asked, "But where will you go after-wards?"

"We'd all like to head for the Province of Canada, but we're not sure yet how we'll get there."

Nate touched her arm. "I'll help you and the others find transportation, and I'll travel there with you. I'll make sure the captain truly won't know which ship you leave on."

"You'd do that for us?"

He looked at her with affection in his eyes. "Yes, I'd do that for you." He touched her hand.

If Jennie guessed right, Nate meant not all of the women, but her in particular. She felt a ripple of happiness.

"Mind, no word must reach the English shores about my whereabouts, either." He was serious for a moment. "I must write and resign, and there's naught to say that they won't con-sider I have deserted my post. If that becomes the case, I may not ever be able to return to British soil."

Jennie grasped his hand tightly.

"Don't fret," he said. "When I left, I had in mind that I'd not be returning home, at least not for a good long while." He squeezed her hand again. "Besides, being exiled near you would not be such a bad thing."

Jennie felt herself turn crimson, but she couldn't keep a smile of delight from spreading across her face. Now that she knew she couldn't return to England, or be with her mother and sisters, she wanted Nate to be a person she could continue to see. Along with Alice and Sarah and Kate, of course.

To calm the awkward feeling that suddenly overcame her in Nate's presence, Jennie looked across the deck. Meadows had reached Coombs and Edwards. After a short intense conversa-tion with them, Meadows headed back their way.

"It's settled then," said Meadows, as he stood against the railing next to them.

"Coombs and Edwards are on side?" asked Nate.

"Yes. They'll stay with this crew until the end of the return voyage, unless they can find an English ship on the island heading back home. They prefer English mates." Meadows grinned. "As far as they are concerned there were no surviving convicts on the *Emily Anne*. We agreed that all were trapped in the hold when she sank."

Jennie nodded and Meadows strode off. Nate gave her hand a squeeze and followed.

Jennie took a couple of steps. Then she stopped short. How exactly would she and the others make it, even if Nate were there to help them? They had nothing but the rags they wore. If they pretended to be stranded passengers, she doubted anyone would take them on board to do chores in exchange for their passage. Even if that succeeded somehow, they had no way of earning money once they reached their destination. Nate wouldn't have any way to earn money for himself, either.

"Wait!" she called to Nate. She ran over to him. "Even if we have our freedom, we have no way of paying our way for our passage or anything else afterwards. We need to think of a plan for that too."

Nate put his arm around Jennie's shoulder and drew her back to the railing.

"Meadows is reasonably sure we'll find a cargo or passenger ship to provide free passage, if we all agree to go to the same destination, and if we offer to help on board."

"Everyone has already agreed to do that, if necessary," said Jennie, "But we have no decent clothes, and what will we do once we reach shore? I'm not sure we can walk around in nun's habits for long, and we'll need food and shelter."

"Meadows and I held something back from the captain," Nate admitted.

"You bartered extra food for ship supplies?" guessed Jennie, glancing down the full length of the ship deck. Where had they hidden these things?

He shook his head. "Not food or goods. Gold coins."

"What?" Jennie's face registered shock. He took her hand again.

"Meadows and I found the rest of Red Bull and Davis' stash in the jolly boat *before* we confronted them about the theft. We kept those coins back," he said with a trace of a smile.

"But isn't that stealing?" Jennie's thoughts bounced over all the things their situation had forced her to do in order to survive – lying, bribery and now stealing. What had happened to all her beliefs and convictions about truth and honour?

"We reckon we were owed wages from our work on the *Emily Anne*."

This was true. "But then that money belongs to you and Meadows," she said.

"We'll keep our share, and we'll pay Coombs and Edwards what they're owed. And let's just say we got a little extra for the perils we endured." He grinned. "Although Meadows was reluctant, we've agreed to share in order to get you and the rest of the women somewhere safe."

Jennie stared at him in disbelief, as he continued. "We'll get you each a dress and some shoes," he said. "The gold was to pay for those things when you landed in Van Diemen's Land, in any case. If necessary, we could pay for passages to the Province."

Jennie gasped back a sob and threw her arms around Nate. "How will we ever repay you?"

"There is no need," he said. "It will be enough that some good has come out of these tragic circumstances. Gently he set her aside and wiped her face with a corner of his shirt.

"Thank you for giving us – me – this chance," she said, clasping her hands. "We may all be able to live free yet."

Nate continued with a warning. "You know getting to the Province of Canada is only the first step. I don't know how we'll all fare once we get there. It's still going to be a hard row to hoe – for all of us. Who knows where we'll end up?"

"I know," she whispered.

"My hope is that it will be somewhere near each other."

"It's my hope too," she said through blurred eyes.

He gave her a shy smile. "You'd best talk the details over with the others. I'm sure your new "mother and sister," and your Irish "cousin" too, will want to make plans with you."

His joke about Davis' mistaken assumption that Sarah was her mother and Alice her sister lightened her mood further. Jennie was pleased Nate had tacked Kate on to her new family. Maybe their group could include Fanny too, if she was willing.

"Land!" Alice shouted.

Jennie joined Alice and stared at the horizon as all the women hurried over to see. Amid the chaos of shouting and clapping, Jennie glanced over at Nate. He gave her a wink.

She linked arms with Alice and Sarah and Kate and leaned over the railing looking across the sunlit, turquoise ocean, sparkling like strands of a diamond necklace.

Ahead of her beckoned a tiny lighthouse on a distant, white beach and the rest of her life stretched out before her. Wherever she ended up, she knew she would hold strong in her own convictions.

ACKNOWLEDGEMENTS

Thank you to Patricia Miller-Schroeder and my writing group members, Alison Lohans, Anne Patton and Sharon Hamilton, for your fabulous critiquing of this novel, while I was in the process of writing it. Your suggestions and edits were invaluable. Thanks to the team at Coteau Books for being as tremendous as ever in the design, layout, marketing and publishing of this historical fiction. A huge round of applause for Kathryn Cole for her expert editing skills that not only pushed my boundaries, but enriched my development as a writer.

Thanks also to Rob Ramage and Linda McDowell for sharing their sailing knowledge and setting me back on course. My apologies to them and to any and all other sailors, or would-be sailors, historians and the like for any grievous errors I've made, or liberties I've taken with the writing of the sailing and shipwreck aspects in this book.

The specific details about female convicts, their crimes and sentences are all based on true stories. Although I studied the historical details of convict ships and life on board during their voyages, not all the materials agreed on the conditions. The times of travel, the size of ships, changes in laws and regulations, and diaries of ship's surgeons gave varied accounts, as did the illustrations available. All agreed that conditions were unbearable and heinous, often much worse than I have depicted here. Of those recorded documents, many were distorted by the hand that wrote them, in order to downplay the horror or actions in creating it.

While what I have written about the convicts is factual, and I sought to be as accurate as I could be in my interpretations of what happened to them on board the ships, there are times, such as during and after the storm, that I used a fiction author's prerogative to interweave what I imagined might be a likely scenario to portray the story in a meaningful way.

I stand by my convictions that this story needed to be told. I believe that the history of societal injustices during the time I've written about is no less atrocious than the horrendous actions that we, in what we consider "civilized" countries, allow to take place against humanity today. I hope in some way the brutality of this story will awaken this and future generations to stop these monstrous cruelties against people throughout the world, regardless of their cultures, beliefs and personal convictions.

Darlene Galandie

ABOUT THE AUTHOR

Judith Silverthorne is a multiple-award-winning Canadian author of more than a dozen books, many of which are children's novels, with one translated into Japanese, plus two adult non-fiction biographies. Her first picture book, published in 2015, is an international award winner. *Convictions* is her first Young Adult novel.

The love of nature, people and history inspire Judith Silverthorne's writing and help shape many of her books. Saskatchewan-based, she travels the world acquiring knowledge of cultures and societies, exploring mysteries, experiencing significant events, and the everyday lives of people, which she weaves into her numerous stories.

As a freelance writer and journalist, Judith has written several hundred articles and columns for newspapers and magazines. Among other writing professions, she has also worked as an editor, researcher, manuscript evaluator, scriptwriter, television documentary producer and arts administrator. In addition, Judith teaches writing classes, and has presented hundreds of readings and writing workshops at libraries, schools and other educational institutions. She has also given presentations at conferences and literary festivals.

For more information about Judith, visit her website: www.judithsilverthorne.ca.

FSC
www.fsc.org

MIX

Paper from
responsible sources

FSC® C016245

 ### ENVIRONMENTAL BENEFITS STATEMENT

Coteau Books saved the following resources by
printing the pages of this book on chlorine free paper
made with 100% post-consumer waste.

TREES	WATER	ENERGY	SOLID WASTE	GREENHOUSE GASES
15	**7,045**	**6**	**472**	**1,299**
FULLY GROWN	GALLONS	MILLION BTUs	POUNDS	POUNDS

 Environmental impact estimates were made using the Environmental Paper Network
Paper Calculator 3.2. For more information visit www.papercalculator.org.